what people are saying about

or to

Ryan Forsythe

and/or

I0624811

Dick Cheney Saves Pai

"There is no way in hell I'm gonna read this, much less blurb it."
    Brian K. Vaughan, author of *Y: The Last Man* and Writer for TV's *Lost*

"I'm afraid I've stopped doing blurbs. I'm not blurbing anyone."
    Stephen Elliott, author of *The Adderall Diaries* and *Happy Baby*

"Congratulations! You made honorable mention in the Creative BFF (Best Friends Forever) Contest. Thank you for participating. Please reply with your mailing address."
    Paris Hilton Entertainment

"   " (*no response*)
    Dick Cheney,* author of *In My Time: A Personal and Political Memoir*

"You are better than google."
    The Way We Sleep, an anthology of prose and comics

"I'm totally going to teach *DCSP* in some class some day in the future."
    Chris Hall, adjunct professor of English

"You should write about vampires because those are big right now."
    Peggy Forsythe, mother of the author

---

* Cue "Dick Cheney" by Lex One, from the Love Earth Music soundtrack *music from and inspired by the novel Dick Cheney Saves Paris*.

Dick Cheney Saves Paris

A
PERSONAL
AND POLITICAL
MADCAP SCI-FI
META- ANTI-
NOVEL

Ryan Forsythe

Love Earth Publications
Santa Susana CA

FIRST LOVE EARTH PUBLICATIONS EDITION
AUGUST 2011

Published in the United States
by Love Earth Publications

This is a work of fiction. Names, characters, places, and
incidents are either a product of the author's imagination
or are used fictitiously. Any resemblance to actual events,
locales, or persons is purely coincidental. Okay, maybe not
totally coincidental, given the subject. But the lawyers want
us to say that anyway. Also, some of the parts about the
author might not be used fictitiously, though that might
depend on your definition of *fictitiously*.

ISBN 978-0-615-49287-2

Cover and book design by Paul Forristal

visit our website
www.loveearthmusic.com

Printed in the United States of America
10 9 8 7 6 5 4 3 2 1

No Paris was harmed in the making of this book.

this one's for you, Dick

consider it a small gift among
half-ninth cousins, twice removed

and for Paris

thanks for the cologne, darling,
but I already have a BFF (my wife)

A Note to the Reader

This book is a work of fiction. Names, characters, places, and incidents are either products of the author's imagination or are used fictitiously. Those items used fictitiously have been exaggerated, re-imagined, and/or placed in an entirely fictional context. Lest there be any doubt, both publisher and author assure you: *Dick Cheney Saves Paris* is not authorized by former U.S. Vice President Cheney and none of it is true. We are certain that *in no way* would the real Dick Cheney behave as portrayed herein,* including traveling from the distant future, ordering two Filet-o-Fish sandwiches (and a small fry), and working closely with Ralph Nader. And we most definitely believe he wouldn't act as the character "Dick Cheney" and release a memoir on August 30, 2011, populated with made-up facts.

It's not real, folks. No need to sue.

---

* Exceptions may include (among other things): voting against the safe water drinking act and the release of Nelson Mandela; encouraging Republican senators to not sign off on the Iran-Contra findings; participating in the neo-conservative Project for the New American Century; and disappearing to a secret location with Donald Rumsfeld to plot altering the traditional line of succession for the presidency—all of which Dick Cheney has done, though presumably not for the reasons listed in this book.

Believing as I do that man in the distant future will be a far more perfect creature than he now is, it is an intolerable thought that he and all other sentient beings are doomed to complete annihilation after such long-continued slow progress.

— CHARLES ROBERT DARWIN
Life and Letters

If reality becomes surrealistic, what must fiction do to be realistic?

— JOE DAVID BELLAMY
Superfiction, or The American Story Transformed: An Anthology

Dick Cheney
Saves Paris

A man sits reading in a chair. Nearby stands a younger man—no, he is a boy. A young teenager, though he is confident, carries himself like a man. Really just a big kid, perhaps a football player or a wrestler. The boy listens as the man rages at his newspaper.

"I tell you, this all started with that god-damn, no-good, good-for-nothin'..."

The boy shrugs his shoulders and tunes out, tries to spin a basketball on his finger. Or rather, the boy *will* shrug his shoulders, will tune out, will try to spin the basketball. For none of this has happened yet. Not unless you are reading this sometime after the year 2791—has some rebel engineer hacked your digital book to outlive its planned obsolescence? If so, maybe past tense is more appropriate: the boy has shrugged his shoulders, has tuned out, has spun a basketball on his finger.

Or: The boy did shrug, was shrugging, had been shrugging—heck, he will have been shrugging. I could go on, depending on when you're reading this: does shrug, will shrug, is shrugging, etc. Let's just say the boy is always already shrugging his shoulders, always already tuning out, always already spinning that damn ball.

This is awkward. Maybe we can do without tenses, without verbs altogether. Let's try...

A man. A younger man, no a boy. Confident. Maybe a football player. Wrestler? Older man with his newspaper. Rage. Words.

"I tell you, son, it all started with that god-damn, no-good, good-for-nothin'..."

A shoulder shrug. A basketball. Still more words. "Son, promise me this. If you ever get the chance to save the world from that godforsaken Gore presidency, that you'll do it." Silence. "Promise me!" A pause. A promise made. A laugh. And then: "You're a good kid, Dick. You're a good kid."

A smile.

Okay, maybe we've moved a little farther into the story. But this is even worse, if that's possible.

You know what? You're a bright reader, you figure it out. Let's go back and begin again, but this time, choose your own tense. If you must, alter the sense as you read, depending on whether you're reading this before 2791 or after 2791, or at the same time the action is happening. Whatever.

So, yeah. I call "do-over."

．　　．　　．

A man sits in a chair, a half-empty beer to his side. Nearby stands a younger man—no, he is a boy. Obviously a teenager though he appears more confident. Perhaps a football player or a wrestler, he carries himself like a man. The boy looks at his ball but is clearly listening as the man rages at the newspaper.

"I tell you, son. This all started well before your time.

Centuries ago, with that god-damn-forsaken, no-good, good-for-nothin' Gore. That's when the party went to shit. I'm almost ashamed to call myself a lifelong Democrat. 'Party of Zee-brox-K04,' my ass."

The man drains the bottle before tossing it at the wall a few feet from the boy's head. The boy is not startled by the pop against the wall or the falling rain of glass. He turns away, but the man stops him. "Promise me, son. If you ever get the chance to save the world from that Gore presidency, that you'll do it."

The boy is unsure if the lecture is over.

"Promise me!"

The boy pauses. "I promise." The first words we hear from him, they somehow defy his stature. A body that exudes strength, confidence; a voice of reserve. Withholding something?

"What's that? Speak up, goddammit."

"I promise!" Almost shouting, before teeth clench tight.

The man laughs. "You're a good kid, Dickie. Yeah. You're a good kid alright."

The boy attempts a smile back, tries to leave before any more promises must be made, before any more questions must be answered.

"Ah, enough of this," says the man. Tossing aside the newspaper, he calls out to the departing boy. "Hey Dick, slow down. Come tell me how school was today. Hey—get back here!"

.   .   .

The teacher stands in the classroom, talking to himself. "Who can help me with this one? How about you, Richard Bruce 'Ricky'? No answer? Okay, well then how about you, Richard Bruce 'R.B.'?"

Richard Bruce "R.B." mumbles something unintelligible.

"What was that, Richard Bruce 'R.B.'?"

"Oh, that wasn't me. Richard Bruce 'Dick' was saying he had something to add."

"Oh, great. Go ahead, Richard Bruce 'Dick.'"

But Richard Bruce 'Dick' is not paying attention. He is thinking of Katie Driscoll, the most popular girl in his small town school of 912,897,300,982. Not that he ever gets to see her, given all the class time she spends at her friend Lynne's house.

"Richard Bruce 'Dick'? Are you there?"

.   .   .

In the future, state budgets will continue to spiral out of control.

The bulk of budget cuts will fall on the education system. With forecasts of record population growth in the coming decades, politicians will worry. One plan, hatched in early 2019, will peg class size to the rate of population growth. Sure, class sizes will only get larger, but at least there will be a plan in place to handle it. Teacher unions will agree, mostly out of fear that if they disagree they will be disbanded by government fiat, as will have occurred in many states earlier in the decade. Plus, they will know what to expect. A few more students each year—at least they have time to prepare.

At the time, the average class size will be 36.9 students. But with an average annual increase to the population of around 3.0% (though it will vary between .14% and 8.6% over the next few hundred years), class sizes will soon grow out of control.

The formula for classroom growth is this:

$$C_x = C_o (1 + y)^x$$

where:

C_o	= Initial classroom population,
C_x	= Classroom size after x years,
x	= Years passed, and
y	= Average growth rate of population

Hence, by the year 2791 we have the following:

$$
\begin{aligned}
C_x &= 36.9 \,(1 + .03)^{(2791 - 2019)} \\
&= 36.9 \,(1.03)^{772} \\
&= 300{,}167{,}617{,}784
\end{aligned}
$$

Yes, average class size will top just over 300 billion. Those reading this in the present may find it hard to believe they will be able to fit so many students in one class. But with technology being what it will be, students can attend classes while eating, exercising, or even shopping on their mallpods.

Sorry, reader? Say again? Oh—you thought when I said

the teacher was calling on the students, that he was actually in the classroom? Oh, ha! That's rich. So pre-22nd century. But no. I thought I made it clear when I wrote, "The teacher stands in the classroom, talking to himself." Oh, you thought I meant... Anyway, compulsory classroom attendance ends in 2107 with 512 students per class, when it is determined that five-year-olds can't concentrate on the lecture. Too much squirming in their seats. Sure, by second grade, kids are broken down enough, er—let's just say "socialized"—are socialized enough to zombie their way through a full day in the big classes. But no, the kindergarteners won't be able to hack it, thus ruining for everyone our once proud tradition of compulsory classroom attendance.

The politicians will revisit The 2019 Plan. Rather than re-consider the population growth equation, they will notice other budget areas they can further slash. One administrator will realize that if they transmit the lecture via students' videophones, they can drop the cafeteria, janitorial, and administration budgets. And by outsourcing the actual teaching, they will further cut costs.

So yes, one teacher lectures streaming live to a class of 300 billion, give or take 167,617,784. This naturally makes it difficult to differentiate among students, especially when schools find it most cost-effective to organize the students alphabetically—the first 300 billion on the list to teacher #1, the next 300 billion to teacher #2, etc. One class could have several million students with the same first, middle, and last names.

Hence, nicknames will be an absolute necessity.

.　　.　　.

"Are you there, Richard Bruce 'Dick'? We're still waiting to hear from you? Richard Bruce 'R.B.' says you had something useful to add."

Dick suddenly realizes the teacher is calling on him. "Shit."

"What? Who said that? Speak up."

"I'm sorry, Mr. Hillyer. This is Richard Bruce 'Dick.' It's just that I'm, uh, feeling sick. I need to unlink for a moment."

"Fine, fine. But hurry back. We're eager to hear what you have to say."

.　　.　　.

As I sit revising this, a story on NPR says a biography of Gandhi may be banned in India because of suggestions he might have been bisexual. The book mentions that he lived with Hermann Kallenbach in South Africa for a while and wrote letters telling Hermann how much he loved him. The book hasn't been released yet, but already it's getting four minutes from *Corey Flintoff, NPR News, New Delhi*.

It's amazing what hints about someone's sexuality can do for a book's publicity.

.　　.　　.

Did you hear this? There's this book about Richard Bruce "Dick" Cheney that suggests he may have been bi-. Or was it sex with horses in Wyoming? I'll have to check my notes.

Oh, and I do of course mean *this* book when I say "there's this book." Don't want you to get confused and go trying to ban some other book.

.　　.　　.

Eleven years pass in the blink of a sentence. Richard Bruce "Dick" Cheney stops by to visit his best friend and the only high school chum he still talks to, Richard Bruce "Kimo" Levernson.

"Say—you wanna head over to Nebogipfel for the long weekend?"

"Oh, I forgot to tell you. My bro is out of town, so he said I could borrow his Filby. I was actually thinking of checking out Firenze 1481 or maybe Nantes 1847. Wanna come with? We could always hit Nebogipfel next month."

Dick smiled. "Dude, you've been wanting to go to Nantes for years, but something always comes up. What makes you think you'll actually make it this time? Let's just hit Natrona 2780."

"Hell, no. High school is a thing of the past. You need to move on, dude."

"Well, Nantes 1847 is even more past."

"You're stupid."

"No, you're stupid."

"I'm not the 28-year-old with the hots for a 17-year-old."

"Hey—Katie Driscoll is not 17. She's the same age we are."

"True," says Kimo, smiling. "But then you don't want to go to Natrona 2791, now do you?"

Dick had been to Natrona 2780 a few weeks earlier, but wasn't sure he wanted Kimo to know just yet. Even though Katie Driscoll totally hated his guts back in high school, 2780 Katie was developing a crush on 2791 Dick. But that's not the type of thing Kimo could ever let him live it down. So he let it drop. "How about Rosebery the middle of next week?"

"Dude, the middle of next week hasn't happened yet. How the hell are we going to know if it's worth our time? Besides, I heard there were some super fine ladies in Nantes 1847."

"Whatever, Kimo. Count me in."

More than spending time with Kimo, Dick looks forward to another weekend away from his old man and his eternal "If you ever get a chance to save the world" lectures. If his dad had so much as one ounce of booze or was anywhere near a newspaper, he was off and running on his favorite topic.

They make plans to meet the next day at the D & P.

.　　.　　.

Fortunately, Gandhi's great-grandson Tushar opposes all efforts to ban the book. And I agree. Just because someone questions another's sexuality, doesn't mean you should re-press their freedom to publish.

But you should definitely give them four minutes on *All Things Considered.*

.　　.　　.

11

If it's true what I say about Cheney's sexuality, he would not be the first once and/or future V.P. with such rumors.

William Rufus de Vane King, U.S. Vice President under Franklin Pierce, was widely rumored to be gay. He and James Buchanan lived together for fifteen years before Buchanan became president. The wigs and scarves Pierce wore prompted Andrew Jackson to call him "Miss Nancy." Aaron Brown called him "Aunt Fancy."

.   .   .

While on the subject of Cheney sexuality, I should note that I'm absolutely not going to mention Lynne Cheney's romance novel *Sisters* or Dick and Lynne's lesbian daughter Mary.

It may work for John Kerry, but let the record show that such cheap jokes and references have been done to death. Besides, in our tale, Mary hasn't been born yet. So why would I mention her?

Nope, nothing to see here, move along, please.

.   .   .

United States Senate Committee on Foreign Relations
One Hundred Eighth Congress, First Session
November 23, 2003

Subcommittee investigation into the vaporization
of Paris Hilton

The committee met at 9:23 a.m. in room SH-216, Hart Senate Office Building, Hon. Joseph R. Biden, Jr. (chairman of the committee), presiding.

Committee Members Present: Senators Biden, Lugar, Hagel, Chafee, Brownback, Boxer, Alexander, Coleman, Nelson, and Rockefeller.

[Partial Transcript]

Senator Lincoln Chafee (R-Rhode Island): Mr. President, I'm trying to understand something. Can you tell us again what day it was that you discovered that the General Electric Epoch Phase Transmitter 5400 DL 1.0 was not actually transmitting individuals to different time periods, but was, in fact, vaporizing these individuals in our own time period?

Senator Joseph Biden (D-Delaware): (Sighs.) Can we please move on. Now, I don't know how many times President Gore is going to have to answer this same question. I mean, have each of us asked him this?

Chafee: If you'll let me pursue this line of questioning, I think you'll appreciate where I'm going. May I proceed or do you need to interrupt some more?

Biden: Alright, go ahead. Ask him what day he found out, so he can tell us again it was June 16.

Chafee: President Gore?

President Al Gore: It was June 16.

Chafee: Mr. President, you say that you were first informed on June 16 regarding Ms. Hilton. As we've discussed, according to the timeline of events, the incident occurred late in the evening on June 14. Now, I don't mean to be presumptuous here. But it seems to me there was a breakdown in communication somewhere. Paris is vaporized and the President of the United States does not learn of it for forty-eight hours. Is that correct?

Gore: It was thirty-eight, senator.

Chafee: Excuse me?

Gore: I learned about it thirty-eight hours after the incident. The incident occurred at 8:47pm on the 14th. I was briefed at approximately 10:45am on the 16th. That's just less than thirty-eight hours.

Chafee: Fine, thirty-eight hours. Even so. Would you like to explain for my colleagues here what exactly was happening on June the 15th? And why it took so long?

Gore: As I've detailed at length, our intelligence officials were examining the recording of the Iranian scientist. The translator was relatively new at the department. Naturally, they wanted to confirm his version. Unfortunately, the agency has few members with advanced knowledge of contemporary Persian.

Senator Richard G. Lugar (R-Indiana): Excuse me, but wasn't it one line of dialogue that needed to be translated? How much knowledge do you need to translate one line?

(Gore consults lawyer.)

Lugar: Well?

Gore: I refuse to answer that based on my fifth amendment rights.

Lugar: Can you at least tell us what he said?

(Gore consults lawyer.)

Lugar: What was it that the good scientist said?

Gore: I believe his exact words would translate as "Oh, my god. They are being vaporized."

Lugar: Oh, my god. They are being vaporized. Huh. Celebrities are being vaporized and the analysts decided right there to slow down, call for a second opinion. Maybe brew up some tea. I'm guessing stop and check their email, too. Mr. President, these are difficult times and as Commander-in-Chief, I hope you are not saying that we as a nation are not prepared for the response that may be needed when an enemy nation vaporizes our cultural landmarks such as Paris Hilton.

Gore: You don't need to lecture me, Senator. You'll recall I saw this coming—I tried repeatedly to shut down the time travel program.

Chafee: You *tried* to shut down the program? Perhaps you should have worked just a little harder, Mr. President. Perhaps we as a nation would not be mourning the loss of Paris Hilton. Or Rob Schneider, for that matter.

Gore: Yes, I should have tried harder. But perhaps if a majority of the Senate had not overridden my veto, including you, as I recall, Senator Chafee, perhaps I would have—

Senator Sam Brownback (R-Minnesota): If I may, Mr. Chairman?

Biden: Please.

Brownback: Thank you. Mr. President, we've been hearing that there may have been conversation between some of the Iranians and the U.S. scientists who built the machine that, uh, vaporized Ms. Hilton. Is it true that a second cousin of Dr. Ferdinand of Lawrence Livermore Lab had a brother who married an Iranian?

Gore: Senators, there is no proven link between the Iranian scientists who developed the faulty time machine, and our scientific community who copied their work piece by piece.

Brownback: What about the letter our CIA intercepted indicating that the Iranians were trying to buy faulty time machine parts from Nigeria?

Gore: Our intelligence community found no basis for that letter. They were deemed forgeries, and poor ones at that.

Brownback: Still, it sounds like our intelligence community was a little unprepared for this time travel debacle.

Biden: Moving on, gentlemen. Mr. President, would you care to comment on why it took so long to notify the national media? It occurred on the 14th, you learned about it on the 16th. The White House press conference wasn't until the 3rd of July.

Gore: When a popular celebrity is vaporized, there is a fine line between the public's right to know and the overriding concern for public safety. You're on the Senate Armed Services Committee, Senator, so I'm certain that you're aware of such considerations, through discussions we've had there. I met with the joint chiefs, I consulted the members of my cabinet. We all agreed informing the public would create a panic. We anticipated heavy rioting in most major urban centers, a run on banks and most financial institutions, dangerous upheaval in the markets, and a resultant increase in unemployment, inflation, and the value of the yen against the dollar. We took steps to shore up these and other important institutions before the announcement.

Brownback: And yet, you still found time to sell your shares of Hilton Worldwide before the press conference?

Gore: As I noted earlier, my Hilton shares are in a blind trust while I serve as President. At no point do I have access to them, nor do I have the ability to buy or sell. It is administered by Grants Global.

Brownback: I guess I find it a little convenient that you would seem to have profited off the loss of Ms. Hilton. Hilton shares were at an all-time high when you sold on July 1st. On July 3rd, after your announcement, the stock plummets. You sold high, and got out just in time.

Gore: Again, I did not consult or share any privileged information with Grants Global, nor did I even speak with them anytime prior to notifying the public on July 3rd. My last contact with them was in February.

Senator Charles T. Hagel (R-Nebraska): I feel this is not getting us anywhere at the moment. If I may, I'd like to return to an earlier topic, that of your attempt to delay the formation of this commission until December. Now I understand your desire to delay this proceeding until after the election. It will play better for your potential re-election if you're not under indictment for murder, Mr. President.

Gore: I did not vaporize that woman—Miss Hilton. The

American people should know the pain in my heart for the loss. And I resent the implication that I would delay anything for political reasons. You may find it hard to believe, but as President of the United States, I am an extremely busy man, and the more I have to come here to answer the same questions from each of you—

Biden: Gentlemen, gentlemen. Can we please—

Senator Barbara Boxer (D-California): Ahem.

Biden: And gentle-lady. Sorry. Can we all please try to calm down. No one is trying to insult anyone here. We are just trying to get to the bottom of things here. Mr. President, I hope you can appreciate that we as a committee have been served with a task, that of uncovering any relevant information. And that means asking questions, lots of them. I do appreciate that some of them may be asking you for personal information, some may be asking questions regarding classified information—

Gore: If you will allow me a moment to respond.

Biden: By all means.

Gore: What amazes me here is that we are focusing so much on what happened to one celebrity, ignoring the larger questions of humanity. What does it say about us as a people that we care so much about one vaporized hotel conglomerate heir, and yet we neglect larger issues that affect *all* Americans.

Chafee: Mr. President, I'm not sure what you're getting at. But perhaps if you could enlighten us with an example of one thing that would affect us more than this incident. I think we'd be happy to hear it.

Gore: Alright. One example. We have recently uncovered information that Saddam Hussein has been meeting secretly with Kim Jong-Il and Rupert Murdoch to develop a terrorism shopping network. Terrorists will be able to buy tanks, sorties, even nuclear warheads, from the privacy of their own underground bunkers. And if they can manage to steal credit card information, who knows what damage could—

Lugar: Now call me a dumb hick from Indiana. (Laughter.) But as best as I can tell, vaporizing Paris Hilton does most certainly affect all people, moreso than some voodoo home shopping network.

Boxer: Plus, Mr. President, if this was something we should be dealing with, shouldn't it have been brought to our attention earlier?

Biden: Uh, if I may interject. I think we're approaching some sensitive areas of discussion. I'd like to move that we discuss this in closed session. No media. A second?

Chafee: Second.

Biden: Any opposed? Seeing none opposed, I now must ask the media to evacuate the room. In order that this be accomplished in a timely fashion without disruption to the proceedings, I move that we adjourn for thirty minutes.

Chafee: Second.

Biden: Alright. We'll reconvene here in closed session at... 10:50am. Thank you, all.

·   ·   ·

When I was thirteen or so, I wrote my first political parody type thing: "Muammar Quadafi Wants to Rule The World" sung to the tune of "Everybody Wants to Rule the World" by Tears for Fears.

I think other seventh graders had different concerns. And perhaps I too should have been memorizing all the words to the Beastie Boys' *License to Ill*.

The next summer, I spent a fair amount of my days watching the Iran-Contra hearings. Why wasn't I off playing M.A.S.K. toys (Mobile Armored Strike Kommand) or quoting *Crocodile Dundee* while sucking on Jolly Ranchers and lounging in my Jams?

Previous summers found me biking the nearby trails or hanging around the pool. And I'm sure I did the same those summers.

Just not until I got my daily fill of the hearings.

.   .   .

I have the report for you, sir, said Lackey #1. He handed it over.

The man quickly glanced over the document. Good god, said the man. This says that it happened sometime between 2001 and 2008.

Yes, sir.

When exactly was it—I need to know.

It's not entirely clear, said Lackey #1. But we've definitely pinpointed it to those coordinates.

Just the time, not even a location?

No, sir.

The man sat back and sighed. Well, then. I hate to do this. But we have no choice. Alright. His entire presidency has to go.

But, sir—that means no Declaration of Universal Peace with North Korea! That means no 'Axis of Hope' with Syria and Burma! Why, this would mean—(gulp)—no mandatory free internet access at all filling stations.

If that's what it means, that's what it means. We have no choice, Lackey #1. It's our last best hope for survival. And if it began with him, then it must end with him.

Yes, sir.

Al Gore must go.

.   .   .

In the past, the record for distance traveled into the future was 20 milliseconds (or 1/50 of a second).

This method of travel was only used by astronauts, as it involves orbiting the earth. The longer a person is in orbit around the earth, the younger he or she will appear relative to a person observing from Earth. Some believe the Apollo astronauts hold the record for longest distance traveled into the future. However, they were only in orbit a few days, which kept them from getting more than a millisecond or two into the future.

The 20 millisecond record was accomplished by astronaut Sergei Avdeyey. He traveled in orbit around the earth for 748 days, at a speed of approximately 17,000 miles per hour. At that rate, Mr. Avdeyey could have eventually zoomed twenty-four hours into the future had he continued orbiting for approximately 8.85 million years.

As can be seen, a process that takes 9 million years to move a person 9 million years and 1 day into the future is not a highly efficient method of time travel. To get one year into the future would take over three billion years.

So the scientists kept looking.

A second method is simply traveling faster than the speed of light. However, it would theoretically take an infinite amount of energy for an object to be accelerated to a speed faster than the speed of light. And that's a lot of energy—perhaps too much to make the trip reasonable for time travel. Heck, even with traveling at *almost* the speed of light to a distant star, then turning around and traveling the same speed back, the amount of energy needed would make the whole thing cost-prohibitive.

A third means is the use of wormholes and what is known as Alcubierre 'warp' drive. A wormhole is a type of warped space-time, permitted by Einstein's general relativity. But let's just say travel through a wormhole is complicated, and leave it at that.

A fourth means is the use of cosmic strings and black holes. But even the scientists don't really want to test them. Because if their theory is wrong, well—you know what they say about black holes.

Other possibilities include time dilation or suspended animation, which, while prohibiting travel to the past, could potentially allow travel to the future. This is the time travel that Walt Disney is hoping to make—should technology be able to revive his frozen self. But this is technically not time travel, as the individual wouldn't be able to make the return trip. It's one thing to be dormant for thousands of years and wake up to a new universe; it's quite another to be able to benefit practically from such an adventure.

For the present, the scientists continue thinking, theorizing, positing, postulating, discussing, debating, examining, analyzing, and attending Star Trek conventions.

But there is another way. Or rather, there will be.

Soon.

. . .

Actually, my first attempt at political humor may have been the year before that Tears for Fears rewrite.

Sixth grade, 1984-85. Ms. Stefancin had us write a report on any country in the world. I don't remember why, but I chose Syria. Perhaps it was assigned to me.

My report took the form of a faux travel brochure. As best as I recall, the cover was something like this:

Visit sunny Damascus!

—just be sure to leave your binoculars at home
(or they might think you're a spy and arrest you)

. . .

Dick and Kimo stop off in Natrona 2780 anyway, to pick up Mr. Hillyer, their history teacher. Sure he was like thirty-five when they were in high school. But now that they are almost thirty themselves, they find he's a pretty fun guy to hang with. Plus, every year they look back it seems their history grades get better and better. It won't be long before they can expect straight A's in history.

"You know, Hillyer. If I hadn't had you for sophomore history, I probably would have liked you a lot more. It's too bad I got stuck with you, huh? Instead of Mrs. Watchett. Or maybe we'd have been friends a lot sooner."

"No—I'm sure I still wouldn't have hung out with you guys back then. I saw firsthand what happened to Mr. G. Ever since I've made it a point to never chill with my students, or their classmates, until at least five years after graduation. That's my self-imposed statute of limitations."

"Whatever you say, Hill."

"I've told you guys before. Please. Call me Larry."

"But, dude. You were always Mr. Hillyer to your face. Or I guess I mean to your voice. We never really saw you. And just Hillyer behind your back. I just don't know if I can get comfortable with 'Larry.' Sorry, but anyhow—how's it been hanging?"

"Oh, you wouldn't believe the week I've had. In fact, it seems that since we started hanging out, your high school selves have been giving me a bit of a hard time."

"Ha ha!" says Kimo. "Maybe we're just jealous of all the time you're spending with us."

Dick knew that in high school he had no idea that they

were hanging out with Hillyer after school, but Kimo's joke makes him wonder. Is it possible that he somehow could have known? Perhaps it really wasn't Hillyer giving them a hard time back then, but Kimo riding Hillyer's ass for fun or something. Hmmm. What would Katie Driscoll say about him hanging out with Hillyer after school?

"Hi, Dick."

There she is! Katie Driscoll.

"Hey, you! I had such a great time the other week—how come you haven't called?"

Kimo's ears perk up. "What's this now?"

"Yes, well, no. I mean. I'm sorry, Katie—I don't know what he's talking about. Kimo, can I talk to you a second. In private."

"Sure thing, bro."

"Um, I'll catch you later, Katie. I'll call you next week."

Around the corner, Kimo confronts Dick. "You've been holding out on me, Dick."

"I know. I should have told you."

"Dude, she's seventeen. You're almost thirty."

"I know, but please do not, I repeat, do not ruin this."

"Let me say it again. She's seventeen. Gimme five!"

"What?"

"High five, Bro."

"Wow. I definitely should have told you sooner."

"Dang skippy you should have. Bitch."

"Sorry. I guess I didn't think you'd understand."

"Well, now you know how understanding I can be. But now you've totally got to forget about her. At least for the weekend. Fine-ass Nantes bitches, here we come! Let's fill up the yogurtank and get on our way."

.   .   .

Up next: another book scandal.

This time it's Greg Mortenson, author of *Three Cups of Tea*, joining the ranks of James Frey, Jayson Blair, Stephen Glass, and others who have taken liberties with the facts in their stories or books. A segment on *60 Minutes* questioned the truthiness of Mortenson's best-seller about building schools in Pakistan and Afghanistan. Author John Krakauer wrote a 75-page article on it.

But we all know that when it comes to fabricating the truth, politicians put journalists to shame. So how come these stories never mention political memoirs?

Or should we just assume that when a memoir comes out, like, oh, I don't know, what's an example? Hmmm. Oh! I got one. Let's say Dick Cheney's *In My Time: A Personal and Political Memoir* (Available August 30, 2011, where fine books are sold). When such a book comes out, should we just assume it will be free of muddled facts and half-truths?

I'll be looking forward to how detailed John Krakauer gets on that one.

.   .   .

In the present, time travel is no longer a thing of the future. It is upon us.

In early 2003, the United States was convinced that Iran had a secret plan to develop nuclear bombs. President Al Gore worked closely with the United Nations to draft a resolution calling on the Iranians to give up their plans. The resolution was passed unanimously by all member nations of the Security Council. The Iranians naturally complied, voluntarily giving up all their uranium. There was nothing else they could do, with the power and strength of several hundred words against them.

Or so the U.S. government thought at the time.

In reality, the words meant nothing. The Iranians were not interested in having a nuclear threat, a nuclear deterrent, or a nuclear arsenal. Nor were they concerned with the nuclear family. For them, the extended family network was vital. For in Iran at the time, as in the rest of the world, it took a village to raise a child.

No, they were developing something even more powerful. And once they realized that enriched uranium had nothing to do with it, they were more than willing to comply with U.N. demands to part with uranium. *Of course, we'll comply with your resolution—especially if it means those pesky weapons inspectors will lower their guard, skip town, and let us continue business as usual.*

It's quite amazing how long they managed to keep it secret. Americans in those days liked to have their eyes and ears everywhere. With their massive network of informants, spies and double-agents, wiretaps, satellites, secret prisons and torture tactics, and—most notably—their dexterity with search engine Google, the government was able to know most everything about most everyone.

Again: or so they thought at the time.

Perhaps the U.S. should have known better. After all, science in Iran has a long and storied history. Significant contributions in nature, mathematics, and philosophy came from Iran—from the discovery of Algebra to medical uses of alcohol. Persians invented the windmill, ornate carpets, chess, venetian blinds, the postal service, chain mail, a uniformly accepted currency, and lasers. And any culture responsible for both the postal service and lasers has got to be considered a force to be reckoned with.

Furthermore, Iran's theoretical chemists and physicists regularly published findings in important journals. Their scientists were at the top of their fields in experimental areas such as polymer chemistry. On top of that, by 2003, Iran had the world's fourth largest population of bloggers. So it should come as no surprise that the Iranians continued breaking new ground, blazing trails in new scientific and technological areas such as the emerging field of bio-time-istry.

But in reality, it was a huge shock. As finally became clear in the transcripts of the Senate investigative hearings, it turns out all entry-level administrative assistants in the U.S. intelligence community were expressly told they just needed to *be able* to find out any information using Google—they were not, in fact, required to find the information using Google, or to even *try* to find it.

What the U.S. didn't know until it was already happening was that Iran was developing a real-life, honest-to-frickin'-goodness time machine.

The latter half of the twentieth century saw the arms race develop and take root, with the U.S. and the Soviet Union stockpiling surface-to-air missile upon surface-to-air missile upon surface-to-air missile. But Iran's work brought the start of the *times* race. Granted, it wasn't much of a race with the head start the Iranians had.

Once they figured it out, they kept going back in time, to buy more and more time. They'd work on it for ten years— say to 2006—and then take that knowledge back to 1996, when, unbeknownst to the rest of the world, their time travel research began. Then they would keep working, but with the ever-growing knowledge they had. Imagine starting that second time in 1996 already with ten years of study toward time travel. But they kept doing this, over and over again.

Of course, the more they did it, the harder it was to keep secret. It was mid-2003 when the Americans finally figured it out. By that time, the Iranians—working nonstop since 1996 —had 397 years of study. Compared to nil for the rest of the world.

Also again: it wasn't much of a race.

·   ·   ·

"Man, the I-5 has got to be the most ass-crack boring freeway in the world. Why'd you take this anyway?"

Kimo was at the wheel, with Dick riding shot-gun and Hillyer perched in the center of the backseat. Cruising down Interyear 5 toward Nantes 1847, Dick popped in their favorite traveling music, *Instrumentals for the Mental* by Generation

Welfare.

"It's balls faster," said Kimo. "You take those lame scenic roads and you're looking at forty extra minutes, easy."

"But it leaves me staring at these god-awful super tankers, making their way to prehistoric times. The fumes are just killing me."

"You know what they say—steal from the poor dinosaurs, give to the rich Americans." In fact, this was the slogan of Texhobo Oil, whose tanker they were stuck behind. Late in 2064, they had abandoned the oil fields, mostly due to there being no oil left in the world, and moved into polymers and finally yogurt. But in 2193, CEO William "Burt" Langerson realized that if they could go back millions of years, fill up some tankers, and then deliver it to the 2060's, they'd be back in business.

"Thanks for picking me up, guys."

"No worries, Hill—it's the least we could do. I mean, I understand not having your own wheels."

"Hey, I've got wheels."

"Sure you do. But bicycles don't travel through time, Teacher-man."

Hillyer was well known throughout Natrona High as that wacky teacher who rode his bike to school. He strongly believed that if he could consume less, he would be doing his part to help the nation become independent of the multi-national yogurt companies. But he was generally open to riding along if someone else was already in transit.

As they rode down through the centuries, Kimo kept his eye on the road ahead, but Hillyer and Dick were able to take in the scenery. Just as they reached the 2100's, the Generation Welfare track "Across the Way" popped on, serving as background music for a montage of famous moments. There was the 2198 inauguration of Canadian Prime Minister Peter "Rock" Mulvaney and soon after, the keosturing of Naza. And—hey, look—it's the Fourth World War in 2179!

"Looks like the U.S. was telling the truth" said Dick, as they watched an asteroid nearly sink Cuba in 2150. "They didn't have anything to do with it."

"You say that because you caught three seconds of it while we were passing by at 200 years per hour?"

"I say that because I just saw an asteroid nearly take out Cuba."

"I'm staying out of this," said Kimo.

"But that tells you nothing."

"It tells me the damn asteroid nearly destroyed Cuba."

"And how does that say anything about any possible U.S. involvement?"

"Because if the U.S. was involved, they would have taken out Cuba."

"Hey, you guys. What's that?" asked Hillyer. They were approaching Vreebul 2111 when something appeared up ahead, just off the side of the road. "I think it's a hitchhiker. Stop. Let's pick her up."

As they got closer, they could see the woman. She held a hand-painted sign that read *DeS Moines 1996 or BuST*.

"Damn, you got some eyes on you, Hill. You must have spotted her from five *years* out. I'm not even sure how you knew she was a she."

"Lucky guess. I guess."

"But I'ma gonna keep driving."

"Would you just pick her up, please?"

"Um, that would be…no."

"I'm staying out of this one," Dick decided.

"She obviously needs a ride and we're going right past where she wants to go."

"We don't have the space. Now drop it."

"What are you talking about? There's the whole back seat here." Hillyer slid all the way to the left, behind Kimo.

"Why would we pick up some roadside hag when we could save the space for a hot chick we might run into later? Think, Hillyer, thi—"

"Will you stop the car? She needs a ride."

"What's your prob—"

"Just pick up the damn hitchhiker!"

"Fine. Fine. I'll pick up the fricking hiker girl. But just know that if we find some piece of hot candy, hag girl is back on the pavement. And you alongside her, *Mr.* Hillyer. Shit-ass. I knew we shouldn't haven taken the fuckin' 5."

Dick pulled over and Hillyer pushed open the door for her. She stared at him a second before slipping in.

"What's your name, sweetie?"

"Call me…Apple pie."

.   .   .

You may be feeling a bit disconcerted over the transition in that last section to the past tense. But now that we've left the present, and are barreling through the past in a Filby XJ, obviously the tense must keep up. Trust me, I know what I'm doing.

I think.

. . .

In the future, time travel will be under control. Totally figured out. But in the recent past, many mistakes were made.

The earliest errors involved engineering. Later lapses included flaws with the force of fluid flow, faulty facilities, setbacks and slip-ups in set-up (not to mention safeguards), problems purchasing the proper permits, mismanagement of marketing methods, and many more miscellaneous mishaps, missteps, and miscalculations.

One of the greatest blunders the Iranians faced was when, convinced they had perfected the technology that would achieve time travel in our time, they sent that first person out.

His name was Mohammed Salami, a member of the special Qods Force of the Islamic Revolutionary Guards Corps and a volunteer for the cause. Though all operations were highly classified up to this point, a grand parade was planned for his return. This would be the announcement to the world. Take notice: We have the power of time travel and you do not. And we are not afraid to use this power. We will harness this technology to bring every citizen of our nation to first world status.

This was a time when celebrities were willing to pay $20 million dollars simply to leave earth's orbit once. Imagine what the Iranians would make from offering short-term guided visits to other eras. And yes, they absolutely would be guided tours. You can't just rent people a time machine for a day and ever expect to see it again. Or if you did see it back the next day, you couldn't guarantee that they hadn't gotten more than one day out of it. Someone would realize they could use it for 20 years and just return it the day after they rented it. Similarly, they would have to be all-inclusive package tours. You can't take 24 people to the Metazoic and have them wandering off to find lunch on their own. Liability is too great. Lunch is included, the lawyers would make sure.

These were but a few of the details the Iranians were working out while awaiting Mohammed Salami's return. Only he did not come back that day.

There was no parade and certainly no announcement to the world. There were only questions: Did something terrible happen to him? Did he get transported to a place where there was not a place for him to be—what if we sent him to a place where there was a brick wall—what would happen to him?

Or what if he saw something so unexpected that he had a heart attack? How would we know if it is the machine or his own machinery—a bad heart, say—at fault for his dis-appearance? And what about the machine itself? Was every piece in its proper place and functioning properly?

Perhaps traveling backward is always a suicide mission, because you are changing the past and thereby making the future different and so there is not a place for you to return to. Once you change the past, the future of that past has not happened yet—you just changed it—so there's no future to return to until you experience it going forward.

Or maybe Salami found a place he wanted to stay forever. Had this decorated military vet made the decision to junk the time machine and flee to a quieter, happier time, perhaps before tanks, missiles, nerve gas, fighter planes? Had he finally found peace? He had a wife and child, but perhaps he was defecting to this other era, his desire to flee Iran greater than his love of family.

In fact, this was the chosen rationalization. An official reason had to be given, always. And thus Mohammed Salami was dishonorably discharged from the Islamic Revolutionary Guards Corps. Not only had his wife lost her dear Mohammed, but being the wife of a dishonorably discharged vet, the law was clear: she was killed with large rocks.

Not knowing what was happening, the team of scientists chose to push forward, try again. Of course, they had a steady stream of volunteers. For success meant history. Everyone in the world would know the name of this person: the first to travel through time. And return.

The second was Mostafa-Hossein Safavi, a strong patriot from a small oasis near the eastern desert basin of Dasht-e Kavir. His comrades had been interviewed and all were clear: There was no way he would defect—he loved his big salty desert of a home just too much to live elsewhere.

He also did not return. Nor did Mohammed-Reza Mousavi from Tehran or Abdol-Ali Hejazi of Yazd. After these four failed attempts, they stopped sending members of the elite Qods Force, and instead took volunteers from the people's militia, the Basij paramilitary volunteer forces.

But after a few dozen of them went missing too, the scientists revisited their work. They pored over every calculation, then over every centimeter of machinery. They took the thing apart piece by piece and reassembled it piece by piece. Everything was in its proper place.

They decided to write out all the calculations by hand. Perhaps in simply reading over them, their brain missed something that their eyes would see.

They stared at the big wipe board, scratching their beards. Finally, one man stepped forward and stared at a spot in the lower right of the board. The marker fell from his right hand as his left hand rose to cover his mouth.

" اوه ،خدای‌ىم آن‌ها‌ت‌ب‌خ‌ى‌ر‌ش‌ده م‌ى ش‌و‌ن‌د ," he said.[*]

.   .   .

In November 2010, former German Chancellor Gerhard Schroeder read George W. Bush's *Decision Points*. "The former American president is not telling the truth," Schroeder wrote.

Let's let's not gang up on Bush just yet: Couldn't Schroeder have been talking about *any* president's memoir?

I mean any president but the first, of course.

.   .   .

---

[*] Literally this translates as something close to "They are being vaporized." But at the time in Iran it was a euphemism for "The shepherd who carries his oldest lamb to the slaughtering table must never choose the youngest blade." It took a while for his colleagues to get his meaning —why was he talking about shepherds? But eventually they get his point.

You remember George Washington?

Old guy on the almighty dollar bill. He *always* told the truth. Age six, chopped down a cherry tree.

Parson Mason Locke Weems describes the scene in Chapter II of *A History of the Life and Death, Virtues and Exploits of General George Washington:*

"George," said his father, "do you know who killed that beautiful little cherry tree yonder in the garden?" This was a tough question; and George staggered under it for a moment; but quickly recovered himself: and looking at his father, with the sweet face of youth brightened with the inexpressible charm of all-conquering truth, he bravely cried out, "I can't tell a lie, Pa; you know I can't tell a lie. I did cut it with my hatchet."

How come we don't expect the same integrity and honesty of all our politicians today?

.   .   .

Sirs, if I may.

Yes. Go ahead.

If we don't act soon, we are going to lose our chance—

No, no, no. From our perspective, 2000 is not going anywhere. It's been history for over 500 years—501.46 to be exact. I think we can afford to wait a few more years to deal with it.

You're wrong, gentlemen. We've got to do it now.

Tell me again, Agent 4. Why it is you refuse to wait for the ballot?

I'll say it one more time. There is no guarantee that if we do wait, that it will even make it on the ballot. Hell, it's almost five years until the next vote anyway.

In time—

I mean, the Irish potato famine, the Crusades, the World Wars—these are all pet ballot measures of some wingnut group or other. But they've all been around for years. You know that unless it's a slam-dunk first-ballot like the introduction of slavery or when Yoko met John, then we'll be expected to wait our turn, like everyone else.

But we have connections with F.R.M. We may be able to sway the counting of the vote. Plus, don't forget the power of effective advertising. When you've got five or nine World Wars, why is someone going to care about erasing any one of them? You've got to *make* people care. Advertising can do that. The WWVI guys have just never taken advantage of that.

I have to agree with my colleague. The Crusades, the potato famine—these guys have never mounted an effective ad campaign. I mean, It's right for the people, it's right for the potato? What is that?

Yes, yes. You're right, gentlemen. The right advertising can help. But at the same time, it can hurt us. I'm not so worried about the issues that have been around. I'm worried about the new old issues that the historians trot out every few years. Twenty years ago no one cared about Princess Di. And look what happened. A flashy ad campaign. Free sneaker giveaways. And boom—they win the vote and her limo never shows that fateful night. I fear, gentlemen, what it will mean to wait.

If we...if we go along with this, Agent 4, would you object to our continuing to work toward the ballot on this issue?

I suppose that would be fine, sirs. That way we at least have the chance that we're operating legally.

No, actually it would still be highly illegal. You'll recall that if our campaign wins, we can't choose the agent. That's still the F.R.M. guys. So even if it wins the vote, we'll never be authorized.

Then why proceed?

If we win the vote and Gore has not been eliminated as of yet—that is, if you, Agent 4, have not been successful, then we will see to it personally that *all* evidence of this present discussion is eliminated. Do we make ourselves clear?

Yes, sirs.

Good, then it's decided. We will proceed with the ballot initiative. And if we can swing the vote before you succeed, then you are history, Agent 4. Get me Hillyer on the line.

You're not going to—

Yes. We have no other choice.

But—

Apple pie time.

.   .   .

Maybe because it never happened. The cherry tree story, that is. That's why we don't expect the same integrity in our politicians.

Parson Weems says of his anecdote, "It is too valuable to be lost and too true to be doubted." But doubt it. I mean, you ever hand a hatchet to a 6-year-old and let him wander off? No, Weems totally made it up. And was there any scandal about Weems playing with facts? Actually, we value the story for its moral lesson on integrity. We fill children's books with its heartfelt story of honesty.

Maybe Weems didn't have the time for fact-checking. George Washington died December 14, 1799 and the book was published in 1800. Weems had to rush to get his tome to the people while still timely.

.   .   .

We the people, in Order to form a more perfect Union, do ordain and establish that the manufacture and fabrication of lessons on truth are even better than the real thing, in particular when such fabrication doth provide for the common Hero mythology, promote the general Bestseller, and secure herein the Blessings to ourselves and our Posterity of blissful ignorance.

—*Done in Convention by Unanimous Consent, In witness whereof We have hereunto subscribed our support.*

.   .   .

In the past, very few countries actively pursued a time travel program.

The U.S. eventually got their act together and found out

what the Iranians were working on. Their spy cameras and microphones caught everything—the calculations, the movement of large trucks through the desert, the long nights scribbling on the giant wipe board.

The U.S. immediately went to work to replicate the technology. Within his administration, President Gore was against funding the program, but he supported it publicly in hopes of firming up his base of liberal electric car-driving movie stars prior to the 2004 election. The word was out: for a mere 100 million dollars, the U.S. would offer a trip to anywhere in the world—any era.

With the proceeds, Gore was able to fix the deficit, strengthen the worsening education system, shore up social security, fund a universal healthcare program, and get homeless people off the streets in popular tourist destinations.

For celebrities, it became the in thing—each trying to outdo the others with their intended destinations. Who was hipper—Madonna with her goal to visit Jesus Christ in 32 AD to warn him about this Judas character? Or Michael Jordan with his plan to bring $10 million to Rome 742 to develop basketball programs for inner city kids? Or Michael Jackson heading to Motown 1968 where he was universally adored?

NBC debuted a new reality TV show, *Only Time Will Tell*, with Regis Philbin interviewing the celebrities both before and after: Tell me, Robin Williams, what do you hope to achieve by bringing comedy to Hitler in 1937? Do you really think that you can penetrate that cold heart and make him more accepting of all people? And later: Now that you've returned, how did you find Hitler? Did you find his humor a touch anti-Semitic?

Many of the "Before" segments were taped and aired, but NBC was having trouble getting the celebrities to return for the "After" segments. Where were they? Lawyers were consulted, lawsuits prepared.

The Iranians watched in horror as one U.S. celebrity after another signed on, paid their money, responded to softball questions from Regis, and went on their way. Their scientific community debated: Is it our duty to tell the Americans they are vaporizing their movie stars, musicians, athletes, comedians, and CEOs? Will we jeopardize our own classified program?

Most agreed: We will keep an eye on which celebrities are going. Tom Cruise, okay. Michael Jackson, yes, fine. Mel Gibson, definitely okay. But if Beyonce or LeBron James or Jennifer Garner sign on, that would be it. We would have to come forward to stop it. After all, all Iranians love Jennifer Garner. Just try having a conversation with one without the show *Alias* coming up. Can't be done.

But LeBron never offered his wad, nor Jennifer her purse. Nor Beyonce or Andre Agassi. So the Iranians never came forward with their secret. They kept an eye on the U.S. while continuing to perfect their own time machine.

In trying to understand what was happening to the celebrities, U.S. communications officer/translator Bobby Thornton began reviewing the surveillance tapes of the Iranian scientists. As the words flowed through his headset, he examined the pages of the official transcription. In the background, a monitor repeated last night's "Before" segment. Paris Hilton would be leaving in the morning to a secret time and place, and not even Regis could get it out of her. Thornton paid no attention to the screen, other than taking his headphones off to sing along as Satanic Puppeteer Orchestra performed the show's theme song live onstage for Regis and Paris.

"Will things change or stay the same?" Thornton sang. "Only time will tell."

Back to work, Thornton read something on the transcript about a shepherd. But the words in his ears were different, quite a bit shorter. Thornton looked up at the screen, then frowned. He rewound the tape and listened again, slowing it down twenty percent. As the words of Iranian scientist Habib Hazhir Yari entered his ears, the pages of the transcript fluttered to the ground. It was June 14.

Thornton swallowed hard and covered his face with his hands as he ran to his lieutenant. "Excuse me, sir," Thornton said, fighting the tears. "I think we just...we just..."

"Spit it out, goddammit"

"We just vaporized Paris Hilton."

"Good god, no!"

Thornton explained that the Iranians hadn't worked all the kinks out yet. There was a problem. They had written $E = MC2$, when it should have been $E = MC^2$. All the work that followed was based on the wrong calculation.

"But that means…"

"Yes, sir. Not just Ms. Hilton—all the others, too. No more *Lethal Weapon* sequels. I'm…I'm sorry, sir."

"Ah, don't worry about me—I'll get over it. But President Gore is going to be pissed. Listen, you're sure about this? I think I'm going to need extra verification. Let me call for another translator."

.   .   .

I've had the same title for this book since I wrote the first draft in 2006. In the process of revising, I thought about these characters and wondered: Was I the only person who imagined some kind of connection between Paris Hilton and Dick Cheney? Using the Google search engine, I entered the phrases "Paris Hilton" and "Dick Cheney." *[Note to Google lawyers: I did not say I googled it, though that is of course exactly what I did. I'm just not saying it.]*

Turns out I am not alone.

On April 9, 2008, Comedy Central's *Root of Evil* pitted Dick Cheney against Paris Hilton to determine which held the title of—yes, you guessed it—root of all evil in the world.

Comedians Greg Giraldo and Patton Oswalt squared off on the topic, with Giraldo taking the pro-Paris position, though perhaps it was really an anti-Paris position, given the nature of the program. Oswalt defended Cheney as root of all evil.

I'll leave it to you and your Netflix account to see who *Root* judge Lewis Black declared as winner/root of all evil.

.   .   .

She's here, sir, said Lackey #2.

Well, send her in.

Of course, sir.

And Lackey #2—close the door behind you on your way out.

So, she said. We meet again.

Yes, he said. Though I'd been hoping it would have been under different circumstances. Something more pleasurable.

Ah, but you called my business line. And since I never mix the two... She licked her lips. You'll just have...to... wait.

Hoo daddy, he thought.

You have some work for me...sir?

He sighed and looked down at his papers. Yes, he said, looking up. Same as before. You don't know me. I don't know you. No one knows anything about anything. Yadda yadda.

Sir—I'm insulted. My past performance isn't enough? You have to sink to remind me of protocol?

This time is a little different.

She frowned. How so? I've seen the results, I know where I'm going, what has to be done. It's not like Sylven 2405. This seems pretty cut and dry.

No, no Sylven. Thank god for that. But let's just say, there may be some competition. And I don't like to lose.

Nor I.

Good. I'll be honest. I didn't want to contact you for this assignment. I was hoping for someone with a little less flair.

Thanks for the vote of confidence.

No slight intended. I know you'll get the job done. But I

also know that your methods are sometimes…unpredictable.

You say that like it's a bad thing.

Fortunately for you, my superiors are more familiar with your results than your means.

You didn't tell them—

No. That's not my place. Besides, they aren't big talkers. Wouldn't have listened to me anyway. But the point is I need there to be no diversion from the stated goal. Can I trust you?

Trust me? Of course not.

I didn't think so.

Hell, can I trust you?

Well…no. Probably not.

So there you are.

Correction. Here we are.

.   .   .

"What the hell kind of name is that?"

"American."

"American, huh? How come I never heard anyone called that?"

"Maybe you don't get out much."

"I bet I'm not the only one. How 'bout you, Dick. You ever hear that name?"

"Nope."

"Hey, Hillyer. You ever heard anyone called 'Apple pie'?"

"Yes, Hillyer. Tell us, have you ever in your life heard of anyone with a name like mine?"

"What, me? Let me think a sec. Apple pie, Apple pie. You

know. I'd have to say—"

"Hey. Why are we slowing?"

"I don't know. It can't be the gas. We've still got half a tank."

"What!? Dammit, Kimo. That means we're completely out of gas."

"I'm jumping out here."

"Hey, don't blame me, Dick. How was I supposed to know half empty actually meant totally empty?"

"Maybe, just maybe, you reject, because it's standard on all Filby XJ's since at least 2780. Doesn't your Dad have an XJ?"

"He has an '81 XT. But I never drive it. You know I stay away from his place as much as possible, so it's not like I need to know when to fill up the damn tank."

"Where are we anyway?"

"Washington DC. I think we just passed 1975, though I don't remember if the numbers were going up or down. We'll have to get a newspaper to check the date."

"Are we going to have to walk? This vacation is so not turning out as I expected."

"Shut up, let me think."

"And why did Apple pie just jump out?"

"What?"

"You said we are completely out of gas and then she opened the door and jumped out."

The car came to a stop and the three men stepped out.

"I don't know. Just help me find some more yogurt so we can fill up and get back on the road."

They left the car and walked into the nearby town, but they had to ditch their Nantes clothing. Because when heading to Nantes for a 3-day weekend, of course you get dressed up before heading out. No one wants to be seen in Nantes wearing a Kinofi or a Lemeksiw—28th century fashion be damned.

There they were in their traditional embroidered waistcoat, felt hat with ribbons, and baggy knee-breeches, when they spied a trio of nitwits in the traditional outfit of the day. Well, Dick and Hillyer used their kyloptigurd on those fellows and walked away in some fine three-piece Armani originals.

"Man," Kimo said. "We looking so fine! Even better than Miss July!"

Hillyer said he needed to check on something and disappeared. But Dick and Kimo stumbled around, found a bar, and drank themselves sick, as their future constitutions were as yet not accustomed to the high grain content of twentieth century alcohol.

They woke up at three in the afternoon and realized they still didn't know the date.

"Where the hell are we?"

"Don't know, man. But I've got a killer hangover. Remind me what you take for a hangover."

"I've always heard more beer."

"Yeah, me too. What are we waiting for?"

Once he had downed a few more, Dick asked the bartender what day it was.

"Today is Thursday, gentlemen. All day long."

"No—what's the date: I need to know the day, the month, the year."

The bartender chuckled. "Sorry to do this. But once you don't know the year, you're cut off. And you're lucky—most of the other bartenders cut you off when you don't know the month."

"Fine—don't serve us. But tell us the fucking date."

The bartender just chuckled and continued cleaning the glasses.

"Come on, Kimo. Let's just go to the liquor store. It'll be cheaper, and besides, we can pick up a paper."

But on the way to the liquor store, they passed a pizza joint. Realizing they hadn't eaten since 2791, they popped in.

"Man, this twentieth century pizza is some good shit."

"As they say, don't know what you've missed, 'til you have it."

Then they drank more beer.

.   .   .

The nineteen-nineties? That sucks.

Yup, and I've got no time to waste. Throw me that shirt, would you?

Catch. You're not taking your stilettos are you?

Never know when they might come in handy. Besides, they're the only things that go with my faux cowhide mini. But I think I'm going to leave the kovy kyupulitres at home.

Hey, promise you'll bring me back something.

What could you want from 1996?

49

I don't know. Maybe one of those early MP42 players that they were known for.

Those don't come around until 2047. No one will even be thinking about them in 1996. The closest thing is an MP3.

Damn, girl. You know so much about the time. I'm impressed.

I have no choice. It's my job. Can you imagine if I was caught talking about the latest Yleuro in 1996. I'd certainly lose my job if I was found out, but it could even be worse. No, I have to know my shit, Weena.

Still, I don't know if I could keep it all straight if my life depended on it. I probably wouldn't know 2071 from 802701.

Give yourself more credit, girlfriend. You know a lot about geothermal nuclear warfare.

Sure, but what good will that do me if I was a proud member of the—

Shhh!

Oh! Yeah, sorry.

Not out loud, Ween. You know better than that. Remember—we don't know who might be listening. Now I am going to finish packing. For *my vacation*. And when I am gone *on vacation*, I will be sure to send you a postcard. It will be so nice to *not be working*.

Yeah. Have a great *vacation*. When will you be back?

I don't know. I've got to see it through to the 2000 election. So I'm figuring I'll be back next Saturday.

Cabron's playing Saturday night, if you're back.

Alright. I'll try to be back.

I'd ask you to call me, but the reception is so damn fuzzy

on those cross-time phones.

I know. Still, I'll try to leave you a message, to let you know I made it safely.

Thanks.

Be sure to water Fifi for me.

I love you. Now give me a hug.

I love you, too. Good-bye, little Weena.

She then walked outside and stuck her thumb in the air. What seemed like months later, Weena looked out the window to see a beat-up Filby heading down the road.

With that, she was gone.

.   .   .

In the future, man will travel to the past in order to destroy the present. Ah, but destroy in a good way. We're talking change for the better.

Drought in Africa? Fly back 300 years and flood the region with seeds and irrigation pipes. Earthquake levels a town? Jump back to planning discussions and move the whole damn town to a different, better spot. Tornadoes, tsunamis, hurricanes, floods, etc.—their effects will be minimized by going back in time and making changes, whether by creating more structurally sound buildings or removing the buildings from the area.

At first, the changes will be greatly appreciated. Families who lose everything in a hurricane will have it all back. A man who watches his dog Fifi sucked into a tornado can enjoy a tornado-less and Fifi-ful life.

But these changes will wipe away people's history with an area, and worse, their memories. That hurricane leveled our ocean front home, goes the theory, but at least we had that ocean view for thirty-seven years. And oh, watching the kids grow up, too! Much better to take the bad with the good than to live in some hick town with no ocean view.

And so, eventually it will fall out of favor. Sure, it may be used for small changes. That street was in a flood plain and if they knew what would happen, the planners could have built it on slightly higher ground? Well, alright then. But following natural disasters, drastic changes will rarely be implemented.

That said, the concept of visiting the past to change the present *will* be considered a brilliant method of battling terrorism. Let the terrorists have their way. They want to blow up a tanker outside of an embassy? That's fine, no worries. Then instead of spending millions to freeze their assets, infiltrate their hideouts, hunt them down, kill them, and spin it for the press, simply wander back in time and kill their unsuspecting great-grandparents. Poof. The terrorists were never born in the first place.

Of course, this will create something of a laissez-faire approach to crime. Police will get lazy, military will stop pre-empting, U.N. peacekeeping forces will stop wasting their time on promoting peace.

Crime will skyrocket, but the liberals will register no complaint. Amazingly, that much less money for police and military actually *will* translate to more money for schools and social programs. Heck—even the Department of Homeland Security will suggest their budget might be better spent on providing affordable health care for homeless inner-city children. No sense spending your moolah on trying aimlessly to stop that one person from taking down a bridge. Because the truth is that you can throw billions and billions of dollars at the problem, and still not catch the one crazy bastard with a chest full of dynamite who's going to do you in. No, much better to wait for it to happen. And then scoot backward a few decades, sack the vandals, and then smack the fast-forward button pronto.

The powers that be will offer a typical "Well, we have to spend all the money in our budget even if we don't need it, or else we won't get it next time" sense to the thing. They'll throw money at all sorts of social programs, even making up new ones.

Pharmaceutical companies will take advantage of the government's largesse, through developing several new "conditions" that will require treatment. To their credit, many such companies will feel they are providing a service to the public. After all, what value is a low-cost prescription drug plan to the citizenry if there is not a wide variety of prescription drugs to purchase? And is it not discrimination to only offer cheap drugs to people with diseases? For the benefit of all those perfectly healthy people out there, the drug companies will help them understand how they too can take advantage of the drug plan. By not being perfectly healthy.

Just a sampling of the new conditions include SBT, EG, and HBO. SBT will be one of the more popular conditions, affecting only those people who bite into something that is too hot before it cools down. Of course Slightly Burnt Tongue can also affect stupid people playing with matches. Apply the topical cream Tongutrin directly to the pain. Elbow Grease (EG) will tend to affect mechanics, both amateur and professional, and is highest among men ages 27-45. Fortunately, it can be treated with several immediate doses of Elboavox. And while Heavy Body Odor (HBO) was actually first diagnosed by elementary school children in the 1980's, doctors were unable at the time to develop an effective drug to combat the effects. It will be available in a lozenge called Odorararal.

Consult a physician if taking any other medications. Please note possible side effects of Odorararal, Tongutrin, and Elboavox include fatigue, dizziness, minor or severe headaches, fever, vomiting, congestion, constipation, miscarriage, impotence, nausea, sleeplessness, restlessness, irritability, cramps, diarrhea, rash, memory impairment, genital warts, intestinal bleeding, and death. Do not take if you are under the age of thirty-six, over the age of twenty-one, generally active, sluggish, pregnant, menstruating, have heart troubles or open sores, suffer obesity, eat a high protein diet, avoid red meat, take Drugippimax™ or Drugippimax Lite™ with new Ortodots™, or have experienced any of the above side effects either before or after taking any of these drugs previously.

.   .   .

From the Journal of Dick Cheney

September 20, 1969

So I woke up from my drunken stupor to discover that Kimo and the Filby were nowhere to be found, all the pizza had been eaten, and I was in the Nixon administration.

Wow, I thought—that was some bad shit. But no—the

more I tried to wake up, the more I realized it was all true. At least I have my own intern now to tell me the date.

So now I'm settling in comfortably in the Office of Economic Opportunity, as special assistant to this Donald Rumsfeld guy. He's a hoot. I think I'm really going to like it here.

Sure it's a different life, perhaps most notably the ability to destroy enemies with a few well-placed phone calls. But I'm getting used to it.

September 26, 1969

Man, can I use a vacation. I know, it's only been a week, but Mr. Rumsfeld has been running me ragged. I haven't had a moment to breathe. I think I might ask him if I could maybe cut back to part-time, just so I could have more time to try to track down Kimo. Don't get me wrong. I love the people and Mr. Rumsfeld especially is a riot and a half. But I come from a time where we have the nine-hour work week and this guy wants me to put in nine hours *a day*.

October 3, 1969

Today I finally had a moment to stop and think. For some reason I got to thinking about my father's words. So often he's taken me aside and said, "Son, if you ever find yourself in a position to bring down the presidency of Al Gore, you do it. You will save the world."

He would then go on and detail how the root of all suffering in the world was in Al Gore's first term. Since he said this in like the 2700's, and Al Gore was like a thousand years earlier (and please note, dear diary: this is what I thought as a kid, now I know that it was actually like 750-790 years earlier), I ignored him.

But now I realize that I am stuck here in 1969 with little or no chance of ever returning to the future. I mean, unless someone comes to get me, that is. I don't think the U.S. gets the technology for time travel until 2007 or so. So it's possible that some day I'll find myself in the year 2000 and then I would have the opportunity to change history and stop Al Gore. And then when I'm growing up and want to be chilling with Kimo or spying on Katie Driscoll, Dad won't have any reason to pull me aside for a lecture.

So there it is. My new reason for existing. Sure, it's not romantic. I'm sure it's not what my obituary will say. But it's the truth. My goal in stopping Al Gore is to keep my old man from bugging the crap out of me some 800 years from now. Even better, if I can actually do this, I might actually make the old man proud. Nothing I've done was ever good enough for you, Pop. But I'm going to change history.

Shit, now I have to do this. It's on.

By the way, I'm adjusting to the schedule a little more. It turns out that even though I'm putting in up to ten or twelve hours a day, mostly I'm sitting at a desk in my own office. So I can nap or eat crackers, and no one is the wiser. Well, except maybe my secretary—she seems to know what's up. But I think those first few weeks, I was stressed from trying to set a good first impression with the boss. And I didn't realize I could have just closed my door and sat around dreaming of Katie Driscoll if I wanted.

. . .

In late 2006, I discovered Miss Snark's blog. Miss Snark is/was a literary agent who disbursed wisdom for writers wanting to get their foot in the door with agents and publishers. She has since stopped writing the blog, though it remains out there in the world.

Miss Snark would hold an occasional "Crap-O-Meter Extravaganza" in which writers could submit their hooks for a book proposal. She would then comment on whether it was any good from a literary agent point of view.

For kicks, I submitted a synopsis/hook for this novel I was calling *Dick Cheney Saves Paris*.

And I got a response.

. . .

Playing bocce and drinking beer in late August 2791, Kimo Levernson invites buddy Richard Bruce "Dick" Cheney to join him for a weekend trip to Nantes 1847. Along the way, their time machine runs out of yogurt, causing them to stall out on Interyear-5. Kimo and Dick stumble around, find a bar, and drink themselves sick. Soon Dick wakes from his stupor to find that Kimo and the time machine are missing and he is in the Nixon administration.

Recalling his father's lectures on the terrible no good Gore presidency—the source of all suffering in the world after national treasure Paris Hilton was vaporized in a freak time travel accident—Cheney realizes he has an opportunity to change history. If he can ensure Gore loses the 2000 race, he can guarantee that 770 years later, he will never have to endure dad's rants.

Excited that he has finally found his life's calling, Cheney dedicates the next thirty years to the task. Will the assistance of alien pinochle player Donald Rumsfeld be enough? Or will he have to enlist both foul-mouthed mob boss Ralph Nader and the secretly Republican robot Joseph Lieberman? And what does the Iran-Contra scandal have to do with any of this?

oh dear dog, this IS funny.
It's not exactly a hook, and dog knows it's all going to come down to the entire novel not just the first pages, but hell yes I'd read this, if only as the antitode to...um... other stuff.

Posted by Miss Snark at **12/29/2006 05:33:00 PM** 15 comments

.   .   .

Hey, honey.

Yes, dear. What is it? Dear?

Wait—I'm reading. Okay. It says here the Gore election is in trouble. Oh, this can't be good.

Come on, what's past is past. Gore was like, what, five-hundred years ago.

Don't you get it? They want to do away with Gore's entire presidency. If Gore is not elected in 2000, then he won't be elected in 2004 either, or if he is elected in 2004, he will have a different running mate—trust me, he wouldn't run with the same VP candidate if he lost in 2000. And if Lieberman is not his running mate, then Lieberman won't be caught up in those robot scandals, so he won't resign midway through Gore's second term and then Hillary will not become VP. And then she probably won't run for president in 2008 and lose in a landslide due to her gender—oh, they were so backward in those days about gender, weren't they?—and so Hillary won't take her free time and go on the motivational lecture circuit, making millions, and so she won't be able to invest in TrinitiCorp, in which case they won't split into Eloi, and Mordocks, and without the split Mordocks will not have a focus on—

Wait. Is this going anywhere? I thought for sure you had a point when you began?

Um, hello? I'm trying to explain. Please try not to interrupt.

What are you talking about? I have no connection whatsoever with Mordocks.

We've got to save Gore or trust me, Mordocks will never raise billions in their initial public offering, and so—okay, okay, I'll skip over some of the minor details. Mordocks becomes—okay, not important—blah blah blah, and then, blah blah blah, and okay, more bladdy blah. And then, Marsden Dash becomes Speaker of the House in 2508. But please trust me, honey, it is all connected back to Mordocks and further back to Gore. Meaning that if Gore is not elected president in 2000, Dash will not become Speaker of the House. And if he is not speaker of the house, then his having oral sex with robots will not matter to the country.

Oh, I see—

And Nancy Chose will not move up to speaker, upon his resignation. Meaning you, honey, upon Chose's resignation for having oral sex with Dash—after it comes out that Chose is herself a robot—then you will not move up to—

Oh. Shit. We need to do something.

Okay, here's what I propose: The election is a week away, and besides, your office advertising budget was maxed by April. But—

Ha! I see where you're going with this.

Your transportation budget has hardly been tapped at all.

Yes! We'll drive around, towing a large sandwich board asking people to vote against the vote against Gore.

Um. No. As I was saying, it's probably too late to influence the people's vote this year. But we can buy more yogurt, and send someone back. The reason people are voting for—or against, rather—Gore's presidency is because they trace all pain and suffering in the world to his administration bungling time travel. It was under his watch that Paris Hilton was vaporized.

That's where it all began.

So if we can stop him from hiring Bill Richardson as his Secretary of Transportation, we should be able to keep Richardson from requesting a 4782% increase in his budget, which should keep them from being able to fund the initial time machine research. And no time machine means no vaporized Paris. That should keep Gore from being listed on the ballot for the 6-years vote, which will save his presidency. And, more importantly, it will keep your assistant under-deputy position safe.

Alright, fire up the T-bird, baby. Set the course for 2003. Al Gore's meeting with Transportation chief Richardson.

Uh—no. We should go back a little further, I think. I'm not convinced the Transportation chief decided anything there—I'd bet it was all written ahead of time and just rubber-stamped then. No, let's set the course for Gore's inauguration.

That far back?

Trust me on this, darling.

Okay, if you think it makes sense.

Trust me.

.   .   .

If Miss Snark liked your hook, you would basically advance to the next round: send the first 750 words or so of the novel, and she would comment further.

Off went my 750 words, which I'll spare you right now. Besides, you've read many of them already, though perhaps not in the same order.

Miss Snark's take?

I'd read this. I doubt I could sell it. On the other hand, who knows. I'd be worried about the freshness factor past 2008 but I'd still probably read it.

I'd want it to be something different than Bill and Ted's excellent White House adventure though.

Posted by Miss Snark at **1/15/2007 02:20:00 PM**

. . .

"I know this sounds weird, sir. But I have reason to believe that future generations will be suspicious of whether you played any role in the Watergate break-in.

"That's ridiculous—I had nothing to do with it. Couldn't have—it hasn't even happened yet."

"I know that and you know that, but unless future generations have some evidence, they're going to think you did."

"Well, tell me this, Dick. In the future, do people believe I'm one of the better presidents. Am I on any, you know, top five lists?"

"No, and it's precisely because of the suspicions."

"So you're saying if I can manage to secretly record instances of me denying that I know anything, then potentially these could be admitted as evidence of me not knowing anything."

"I think so. At least if I remember my history correctly."

"Well then, let's go shopping."

Nixon took Dick to his favorite electronics store and showed him a Sony tape recorder. "How about this one?" Nixon asked.

"Oh, the 800B," the clerk jumped in. "That's one of our top models."

"He's right," noted Dick. "In 2791, I have the 800G and it works like a charm. Of course that's before next year's vote that might do away with monopolies, so it's quite possible that Sony in 1969 will no longer have a monopoly on such tape recorders, so perhaps things will turn out different in the future as we come to know it, as opposed to the future I've come to know."

"Dammit, Dick. What the hell are you talking about?"

"Perhaps there will be a few other companies making tape recorders and the competition will drive Sony to do something other than update their 800B every 230 years.

"Fine," said the president. "We'll take ten of these."

"Grab some of those lavalier microphones, too."

. . .

Note those words from Miss Snark: *past 2008.* I had a deadline. And I missed it.

Please note, especially if you happen to run a publishing company, that this is not a common experience for me. I generally adhere quite well to deadlines. Just ask any and/or all bosses and/or teachers I've ever had.

But, as they say, life happened. A new baby. Changing jobs. Travels. Et cetera and so on. By the time I was settled and ready to focus on my writing yet again, the world had a new world leader supreme, Paris Hilton had been usurped by Lindsay Lohan and then Gaga in the celebrity yellow papers, and then Charlie Sheen was somehow winning, and no one save a few thousand liberal tree-hugger Alternet subscriber types and maybe several million Europeans were interested in Dick Cheney.

Here's one response from *past 2008*:

"Thank you very much for your query, and for your

patience in waiting for a response. Your idea seems interesting, and I have no doubt there are readers for it out there. However, our press is a boutique publishing house, and that means its list is shaped entirely by my whims.

"Unfortunately, *Dick Cheney Saves Paris* does not sound quite like something I am looking for at the moment. It is a matter of my rarely explicable taste rather than a comment on your talent or the potential of your work."

No, the message doesn't explicitly say the idea is "Yesterday's news." But that's the sense I get.

.   .   .

As the months passed, Dick periodically stopped by to check on the microphones. See how they were working out.

One day, Nixon was talking to Haldeman and both stopped when Dick came in.

"Hello, Dick."

"Mr. President, sir. Bob. What are you guys up to?"

"Nothing, don't worry about it."

"Hey, don't think I don't notice you never include me in your conversations." Dick was angry. For the longest time these guys would shut up whenever he came around.

"Well," said Haldeman. "I think we have very different interests. After all, we want total world domination, but you —what was it you wanted to do again? Your little pet thing? I'm sorry, I keep forgetting. Tell me again."

"I'm here to keep Al Gore from becoming president, so I can prove my worth to my father."

Nixon glared at him. "What the fuck are you talking about?"

Cheney sighed. "Jesus Christ. How many times do I have to explain this to you two? If I've said it once, I've said it a hundred—"

"Don't be an asshole, Dick." Nixon pressed a button on his desk. "Rose, can you get Dick here a good strong drink. And get me one, too."

"I made a promise to my father. I must stop Gore."

"Raisins! I need raisins!"

Dick was confused. "What?"

"He wants some raisins," Haldeman said.

"Dick's outta his fucking mind and I can't have raisins. Somebody's going to pay for this."

"As I was saying. I'd appreciate if you wouldn't just shut up as soon as I walked in the room. Is that too much to ask?"

"You're right. We're not respecting your feelings. And for that I apologize."

"Thank you. And how about you, Mr. President."

"Yeah, yeah. I'm sorry."

"Thank you, sir. I know that was very hard for you, but I want you to know I truly appreciate it. Both of you—it means a lot."

"Can you please go now?"

At this point, Dick left, but he was curious as to whether Nixon and Haldeman were talking about him, so he drained his highball and held the open end of the glass to the door and the other end to his ear. This is what he heard:

"That's innovation for you, Haldeman. See what you can

do about getting Cheney a promotion. I need to reward people like that."

"Yes, sir. Of course, sir."

"Make him my deputy assistant. Oh—and let's delete this conversation from the tapes—I don't want future generations to think I have anything to do with whatever he has against this Gore kid. That's his thing, not mine, and as such, it has no place on my tapes. Delete the last eighteen minutes or so."

"Yes, sir."

"Now what the hell were we talking about?"

.   .   .

Sir, the latest vote is in, said Lackey #3.

Hell, I thought we just had an election. Has it been six years already?

No, sir. You're just visiting us five years in the future. You were running low on office supplies, so you popped here for Sharpies and Post-It notes.

Yes—well which is it? The Western Schism of 2419? Maybe the potato famine has finally taken it. Ha! I jest.

No, sir. It's the 2000 election of Al Gore over John McCain.

You're shitting me, right?

No, sir. A huge advertising push the last week won it. Great campaign—

God, I hate this job, he said.

Don't you want to hear the jingle? It's quite catchy. It goes like this. Can't get up from down on the floor? Stay there if you stay with Gore—

Fuck. Fuck!

Sir? Isn't this good news? They'll take care of Gore. Isn't that what we want? I mean, those guys never fail.

Lackey #3, I just sent an agent back to deal with Gore. And she never fails either. Which means one is going to get in the way of the other. And if it's mine that gets in the way of F.R.M., well, let's just say they're not going to be too happy.

Can we bring her back, sir?

No. She knows the rules all too well. No communication. We won't hear from her until the job is done.

Oh.

And besides. She's the least of my worries right now. I don't have much time to stop them from eliminating…me.

.   .   .

For several years, the novel remained in my computer's hard drive, unnoticed, unconsidered, unloved.

Until this past January, that is, when Simon & Schuster announced that Dick Cheney's *In My Time: A Personal and Political Memoir* would be released August 30, 2011.

I began thinking of my Cheney novel. What if I could revise and release my book on the very same day? Maybe it's time. After all, this could be the only day for the rest of my life that the book might be considered timely.

I'd have to think about this.

.   .   .

In the present, there is ongoing debate on the many issues surrounding time travel.

The Iranians realized they had a philosophical can of worms, just on one topic. Consider the issue of immigration: what if people could immigrate across time, such as across China before the Great Wall, across Germanys before the Berlin Wall, or across the U.S. border any time? Would they lose the bulk of Iranian citizens to Los Angeles 1984?

But there are many other questions being examined. Consider just a few:

Should time travel be something left to only the most well-off, people who can afford their own time machines, or should it be part of the public transportation system? If it is the latter, how much money should the nation invest in time travel infrastructure? Should there be senior discounts or monthly passes? Should food stamps be accepted for time travel?

Should there be a tax on time travel, and how would it be collected? How would it be enforced?

Should individuals, upon their death, be allowed to bequeath their estates to themselves at an earlier point in time? If so, should the state be responsible for carrying the deceased's effects to the person in the past, and for telling the person, "You just died—here's your belongings"? Or would it be up to the deceased to have planned that out in advance?

Should individuals be able to travel across the borders of time to buy cheaper prescription drugs?

Should history teachers be required to teach students the history of the future, or continue to limit coursework to past history, in which case students might not be as prepared as citizens of an increasingly global society?

Should CEOs be required to include the actual future cash-out value of stock options when they list the company's overall net worth?

Should death row inmates be allowed to travel to the past and stop themselves from killing?

Should a pregnant teenager be allowed to return to the past and decide not to have sex, thereby effectively aborting her child, without notifying her parents? Or should the child be required to gain parental consent? If so, what does it say about our society once we are effectively requiring parental consent for a child to *not* have sex?

Should the government be allowed to extradite prisoners of war to other centuries, such as medieval times, when less humane torture tactics were considered humane? What if the prisoner has knowledge of an imminent terrorist attack?

Should there be a universally accepted driver's license for time travel?

Should there be age restrictions on time travel? After all, we have them on vices such as alcohol, cigarettes, gambling, pornography, and voting.

All important questions that require careful attention.

The U.S. will strongly insist that regardless of any conclusion regarding these issues, once the technology is developed, it must be used primarily to protect us from danger. They will view time travel as primarily a weapon of defense, against natural disasters. Against terrorism.

Ultimately, it will be determined that this approach—

going back in time to destroy unseemly things—is a good idea, but there will be concerns as to who gets to determine what is unseemly. Should the U.S. be Time's police? Because the Americans just might have a different opinion than France or China. And how often should this be allowed? If the Americans are changing history every week, it might not leave time for other countries to get their affairs in order.

It will be left to a U.N. committee to sort it out. The end result of which will be the every-six years vote. Every six years, everyone in the world can vote for what they deem the most unseemliest historical event.

This conclusion will not be without controversy, with smaller nations arguing that large countries like India, or even countries with lower voting ages, could stack the ballot. So there will be compromise: each and every person will get one vote to determine their own country's vote. That is, a majority of votes by the people of a country determine that country's vote. But each country will have but one vote. The U.S. is equal to China is equal to Lichtenstein. Is equal to Argentina plus Malta minus Fiji divided by France. And the event that receives the most votes wins. Or loses, as it were.

There will be additional controversy over whether additional votes should be granted to countries that no longer exist. For a temporary fix, it will be decided that only currently existing countries will get a vote, though it won't necessarily have to come from the current head of state. If England wants Queen Elizabeth or even Maggie Thatcher to cast the vote from England, that is fine. If China would rather have Chairman Mao present the vote from China, that too is acceptable. But the question will be revisited in time.

The one thing everyone will agree on, however, is the timeline: six years gives enough time for careful reflection, as well as plenty of time to develop and implement multi-billion dollar non-stop around-the-clock in-your-face ad campaigns, targeted primarily at the youngest voters, to promote eliminating one event or another.

.   .   .

From the Journal of Dick Cheney

February 8, 1973

So it has become an obsession. I've been thinking more and more about how to get from here—the Nixon administration—to there: Stopping Al Gore from winning the 2000 election and becoming president. I think I've got it.

What I'll do is hang out here a bit, working as Rumsfeld's special assistant in the Office of Economic Opportunity, then slide over to assistant director with him at the Cost of Living Council. Then when Nixon resigns, I'll cozy into the Ford administration by getting Rummy to name me his deputy chief of staff, and then when he gets the Secretary of Defense gig, I'll be set to replace him as chief of staff.

When Ford loses, I'll run for Congress in some small state —say Wyoming—where I can be the sole congressperson [*Note to self: develop a biography that involves growing up there in the '40s and '50s and not being born in Sebald 2754*]. Eventually I'll work my way up to head of the House

71

Republican Conference and then Minority Whip. From there, in order to get me some street cred, I'll position myself for a cabinet position under George Bush.

I had thought education might be interesting or even environment, but if I truly want to stop Gore, I'll need some real munitions like I could get from the military. So I'll worm my way to the position as Secretary of Defense, which I can hold until Bush loses his bid for a second term. That's all I've worked out so far, but that will take me clear to 1993.

Hmm, what then, what then… Think, Dick, think.

February 12, 1973

I got it! I'm going to get myself a position as CEO for a large corporation, something to do with oil, so I get the business connections to go along with my government connections. And then when McCain runs in 2000, I'll be able to stop him from losing to Gore by tossing bijillions of dollars at his campaign. Heck, that ought to influence something. Because if anyone is going to take an unlimited amount of campaign finance, it'll be McCain.

Huh. This is all so crazy, it just might work. I can't wait to see the look on my father's face when he finds out that I saved the world! No more lectures on bringing down the presidency of Gore—probably no more lectures on being a worthless slob. It's like a two-for-one. Buy one, get one free. Two-for-Tuesday. Boo-ya!

Damn, I better get going—I've only got the next 26 ½ years to pull this all together.

February 13, 1973

Tomorrow is Valentine's Day and once again I will be without a Valentine. I probably wouldn't have one back home —I'd probably be splitting a case with Kimo right now—but who knows? That last time I saw Katie Driscoll 2780, she mentioned she had had a great time.

Heck, right now I'd settle for Lynne Vincent.

February 14, 1973

Craziest thing happened. I wrote in my journal yesterday that I'd settle for Lynne Vincent and when I woke up today, there she was! She says we've been married for nine years and have two kids!

I feel I must have somehow slipped into a parallel vortex in time. This will require much study, probably hundreds of scientists and a huge laboratory. But hell—it's not like I don't have the budget of the U.S. government to work with.

February 15, 1973

Learned it was Rummy playing a joke on me! No parallel universe. Apparently he'll get his own time machine in 2011, and just for kicks he'll pop over to my place 1975 when I'm not there and read my journal entries. Upon seeing Lynne's name, he'll jump to Natrona 2780 and ask if she wants to play a trick on me. I tell you, that guy is a hoot. A hoot!

Part of me wants to ask Rummy if I could borrow his time machine to go home, but I need to think this through. I mean, I love my life back in the future. As they say, home is where the heart is. But I kind of hate that life, too, if that makes any sense.* Partly it was my circumstances —those lectures from Dad, etc. But partly it's who I was. I had no drive, no real purpose—something I definitely have here, even if it is to please someone in the future that I'm in no hurry to rush home to see.

I do miss Kimo and it would be great to see him back home,. But then I'm not even sure he would be there, given that the last time I saw him, he was passed out in 1969.

Maybe I should be thinking of more than just myself— this is the suffering of the whole world we're talking about.

Shit. I've got to stay and see this through, no matter what it takes. There's too much at stake.

February 21, 1973

Back to the Gore thing. I know, I know, dear diary: My favorite topic. Well, excuse me if it's on my mind.

Part of me thinks I could just take the easy way out and just track down Al Gore and destroy him right then. Here in 1973, he must be what—just out of high school? He'd be an easy target—I could probably sit in a car outside his house and pick him off with one bullet. But aside from the fact that I have people to do my dirty work for me, so it would never do to sit outside some punk high schooler's house—aside from that fact, is that I really have nothing better to do for the rest of my life while I wait and hope for someone from the future to come and get me and take me back to my own time. I mean, if I just off him now, what will I have to live the rest

---

* Cue "Lost in a Hole" by Jeph Preece, from the Love Earth Music soundtrack *music from and inspired by the novel Dick Cheney Saves Paris*.

of my life for?

Hmm, knowing that if I took the long way around—instead of just offing him today—I have 27 years to prepare —well, that gives me many many ideas. Maybe I could try them all.

Okay, okay. You got me, dear diary. You know me too well. The reality has nothing to do with offing high school kids or that I have nothing else to do. The reality is that things are going really really well with Lynne and changing things now might jinx it.

I know it's only been a few weeks, but I could see this really working out and I don't want to screw it up. I think she may be the one. And I don't care if I haven't really dated anyone else.

March 7, 1973

Lynne and I talked it over and she says she wouldn't mind staying here permanently, rather than going back to Natrona 2780. Now we just have to develop a past for her, which shouldn't be too hard as yes, one again, I've got the whole U.S. government working for me. Cool.

Also, today I was buying some more crackers when I bumped into this guy. He looked familiar so I asked "Do I know you?" But he acted confused and just shook his head. Later, I stood behind him in line when he was paying with a check. The name on the check was Shep Nirtley.

Shep Nirtley...Shep Nirtley. I know that name from somewhere. But where?

I've got a bad feeling about this.

.   .   .

The week after hearing about the Cheney memoir, I learned Eric Martin and Stephen Elliott were releasing *Donald*, a fictional depiction of Donald Rumsfeld caught in his own prison system.

Their book's release was timed to coincide with the February 8 release of Rumsfeld's autobiography, *Known and Unknown*. Though actually they claim it is a coincidence that their book and Rumsfeld's book appeared the same week. Interesting, I thought. So they had a similar idea. Maybe the world is ready for this sort of thing.

I felt a kindred spirit with Elliott. A few years earlier, I was fortunate enough to read an advance copy of his book *The Adderall Diaries*. To get the word out, he made his own lending library, mailing out 40 or 50 copies of the book to interested readers, who each had one week to read and then mail on to someone else. Over 400 people had the chance to read and pass on his book, at the cost of media mail postage. Here was someone not afraid to take chances and try new things in publishing.

I immediately ordered a copy of *Donald* as a birthday present for myself. On my birthday a few days later, while awaiting the book's arrival, I emailed Stephen to describe my project. Would he consider blurbing my book?

I was excited when I opened my Inbox later that day and found an email from him!

I thought of putting his words on the cover. Maybe his name really big and bold:

STEPHEN ELLIOTT, AUTHOR OF *HAPPY BABY* AND *THE ADDERALL DIARIES* SAYS:

And then I'd put his words really small: *"Nice to hear from you. I'm afraid I've stopped doing blurbs. I'm not blurbing anyone. Sorry."*

Do people actually read cover blurbs anyway?

New plan: be the first author to fill the back cover with quotes from famous people saying they don't do blurbs.

.   .   .

I know you just checked the back to see if there are any blurbs there. Don't feel bad. I even checked myself.

Just don't forget to check the very first page of the book.

.   .   .

A crime is a crime, a dime is a dime—

Excuse me, sir.

Oh, Jimmy. There you are—have you heard the new Versa? Fucking brilliant. A rhyme is a rhyme and I be on—

Sir, you said to notify you when the vote came in. The chosen event was the victory of Al Gore in 2000.

Fucking A! That's great.

I don't see how—

You don't see? This changes everything. It's just the chance we need against the dipshit wankers.

What, for McCain to win? As far as we're concerned that's just slightly worse than Al Gore. Tweedledee and—

No, asswipe. The event that will be eliminated is Gore

77

winning. Simply removing a Gore victory does not guarantee a McCain win in its place. No. This is our chance.

I still don't get you.

Listen. What if taking away a Gore victory meant bringing one, not to McCain, but to someone else? What if all the nutsacks and queefburgers that *would* have voted for Gore instead voted for someone like…me?

Sir, the F.R.M. handles this. They've probably already sent someone back and I hardly think they would help us. They probably financed most of the campaigns to vote against Gore in the first place, just so they could bring victory to their party of favor.

Yeah. But perhaps we can beat the dickwads to the punch.

What are you thinking?

If they do eliminate Gore, all the progressives will be looking for a candidate who believes in gun control, a progressive tax system, more money for education and less for military, less environmental pollution, increased regulation of business, campaign finance reform—shit like that. Does that sound like a fucking Republican?

You don't mean—

Yes. The absence of Gore will create a vacuum. And I will fill that void like a bitch.

But, sir, you don't believe in any of those things.

That's true. Taxes, gun control, education, financial regulation. Punk-ass hippies.

So why would anyone vote for you?

I don't know. Maybe I can make 'em think I'm for all that bullshit. Regardless, I'm going back.

But what if they don't eliminate Gore—what if they have other plans, and there is no void? And what about our work here? Everything we've built? The drugs, the cars. The whores? Sir, you have an empire here and you want to throw it away?

The fuck you know about empire, Jimmy? We spent decades developing this. But do you have any idea how much time I've wasted on blow and pussy? But shit, if I could be president. It'd be like going from fucking crime overlord to master of the bitch-ass motherfuckin' universe! Why I'd have the backing and support of the U.S. Government. Aw, yeah. A dime is a dime, a crime is a crime, and I be on mine—

Well, give my regards to DC 2000, sir.

No, my boy. You have much to learn. I can't just show up in 2000 and expect to win a presidential election. I'm going to have to go back much further, maybe all the way to the 1960's. Heck, I'll probably even have to run a presidential campaign or two prior to 2000, just to get the hang of it.

You really think you can win a presidential election?

Of course I can win. I'm Ralph motherfuckin' Nader.

. . .

In the past, people lived in fear of terrorists. But in the future, terrorism will not be so terrible.

With the program to go back in time to eliminate the grandparents of terrorists, terrorism will lose its ability to terrorize, and hence it will lose its appeal. And also its stigma. Terrorists will come out of the closet and develop support networks. The 12-step Terrorists Anonymous will become popular in major cities, as will Suicide Bomber Hotlines. In fact, programs such as these will be some of the primary recipients of the money formerly used for fighting against terrorists. Terrorists Anonymous, and M.A.T.T., the Mothers Against Tipsy Terrorism, will become the most well known, but others will prosper as well, such as Terror for America which will train former terrorists to teach in low-income schools, while also forgiving any student loans they may have incurred.

No Longer Future Parents of Terrorists (NLFPT) will be a dating service that will match people whose spouses were killed in the quest to stop future terrorists, widows and widowers who never had the chance to have a son or daughter, let alone a terrorist grandson or granddaughter. Or rather, never had the *second* chance, as they did have the kids at some point in time.

Of course, all the support for the terrorists will have its own backlash: How come the terrorists don't have to find real jobs? Why is it that the terrorists can just cross our borders without registering or getting a driver's license? Do they even pay taxes? If they want to live here, the terrorists should have to learn English. The terrorists want to have their cake and eat it too. My daughter's terrorist sister in Terrorist Big Brothers/Terrorist Big Sisters is teaching my little girl to create incendiaries. And so on and so on.

If anything, it will be believed by those of the extremist middle that such programs create more terrorists. After all, what motivation will a terrorist have to find real work when he or she could hint at blowing up a school and then live on public support?

Soon after the backlash begins, most terrorists will have to live in fear for their lives. Even people who have never considered committing an act of terrorism in their lives will have to stay off the streets, as more and more average citizens are mistaken for terrorists. Terrorists will go from being the feared to the living in fear. It will be a sad day for these formerly proud people, when they must resort to hiding among us, living on food stamps.

In the end, many of the programs will be dropped when fiscally conservative Democrats are returned to power. And the terrorists will move to Canada in order to regroup and plot their next strategies. And of course to take advantage of universal healthcare.

.   .   .

"Hillyer!"

"We meet again, Dick."

"No—you're wrong on that. We meet for the first time."

"What?"

"We will know each other in the 2770's. You're my History teacher. But it is now 1982—so we haven't met...until now!"

"Well, what about when we arrived in 1969—wouldn't that have been the first time?"

"It would have. Except, we already knew each other on the ride down, so at no point were we *meeting*, as it were. I would say this is our first meeting."

"Fine. Point taken. Can we start over, please? I fear the moment has lost its dramatic tension."

"What? Oh. Sure." Dick pauses. "Hillyer!"

"We meet…uh, for the first time. Congratulations on your re-election, Dick. Third term now, huh? And Republican leader on the House Intelligence Committee. Very impressive. If I didn't know you better, I'd say you had some ambition in you."

"Well, you don't know me better—we've just met for the first time. Or have you already forgotten?"

"Fine. Let me rephrase. If I wasn't so familiar with your work, I'd say you had some ambition in you. You see, Dick, I am familiar with your work. 'Abraham Lincoln: A Very Brave Man' seems to ring a bell. Yes, I think to the tune of a C-, it sounds familiar. Though I'd suppose you might say it hasn't been graded yet. Not for another seven-hundred years. So perhaps when it does get around to receiving a grade...hmmm, let me think. Oh, yes...perhaps a solid F might be appropriate."

Dick gasped. "You wouldn't."

"Oh, I would. Unless..." Hillyer smiled.

"Man, I can't believe it. I'm going to fail History! Shit. My dad is going to kill me—that's his favorite subject, you know. I mean—"

"Stop, stop. You were supposed to say 'Unless what?'"

"What?"

"No—'*unless*' what?"

"'*Unless* what' what? I have no idea what you're talking

about."

"I said 'Unless…' and that's when you should have said 'Unless what?' and then I would have told you how to save your History grade."

"Oh! Um, *unless* what?"

"Close enough. Dick, from your work back in the Nixon administration, you know how important it is for a president to have just a tiny bit of freedom to operate without pesky senators or congressmen interfering in his everyday business. Rather soon, you will discover that our heroic and patriotic president—or perhaps I should say he doesn't know about it at all—has created a privately funded offshore foreign policy initiative, designed to help our dear friends, the Contras in Nicaragua. Congress will investigate, and of course they'll want to question everyone—from the lowest level military officer all the way up to the White House."

"Well, if we are helping our friends, why is there an investigation?"

"Because the enemy of our friends is our enemy. That's all you need to know, Dick. But with your leadership, you can block these nasty Democrats from questioning people like our good friend Vice President Bush. I also want you to ensure that not a single House Republican signs the committee's final report. The committee will want to charge the administration with disdain for the law and deception. But you will see to it that Republicans issue their own report. And of course this report should claim no wrongdoing on the part of the administration."

"So you're saying that if I fight congressional limits and

oversight of presidential authority, and if I fight against the investigation of this secret program, you'll give me the C in History."

"C? Oh, Dick, you have much to learn about negotiation. If you can accomplish all that, it'll be worth an A, perhaps even more. But I'm willing to compromise on this. Hmmm— you say C and I say A. Alright—I'll give you a B. But that's the best I can offer."

"Alright, Hillyer. I'll do it."

"Oh—and Dick. Until you graduate Natrona, please call me *Mr.* Hillyer."

.   .   .

Apparently nonfiction authors sometime grow to identify pretty strongly with their subjects. So does it happen to fiction authors writing about real people?

Me and Dick Cheney?

Well...maybe.

In learning about him, I've come to find that we were both born under the sign of Aquarius. Both married Leos. Both one of three children, both with a brother named Robert. Neither of us served in the military.

And how about this: Dickie Cheney's mother's maiden name was Dickey. His parents were a Dickey and a Cheney. Dickey and Cheney—Dick Cheney. My mother's maiden name is Ryan. Yup, my parents are a Ryan and a Forsythe. Ryan Forsythe.

Okay so it's not an exhaustive look, but you can see that

it's almost like we're blood brothers.

I get you, Dick Cheney. You had me at "Go fuck yourself."* That Senator Leahy deserved it. Standing there all smug on the Senate floor.

.   .   .

Interviewer: Mr. Levernson, before we begin, you should know that we ran a background check and there is no record of anyone named either Kimo or Levernson living where you've claimed to have lived for the past several years. Now, I'm inclined to say this interview is over right now.

Kimo: But I can totally explain—

Interviewer: Hold on, hold on. Let me finish. I was going to say, I'm inclined to say this is over right now. But. But I'm intrigued enough by some of the other things on your resume, that I'm willing to hear your explanation of who you are and where you've been. Please shed some light for me on just who you are and where you are from.

Kimo: I've been living in the greater Metropolitan Washington DC area for approximately—

Interviewer: Snore.

Kimo: Sir?

Interviewer: Snore. As in, you're putting me to sleep. Spice it up if you want another minute of my time.

Kimo: Alright, you want the truth? I've come here from the

* Cue "Go Fuck *Yourself*, Cheney!" by +DOG+, from the Love Earth Music soundtrack *music from and inspired by the novel Dick Cheney Saves Paris*.

future. I was living in the year 2791 and wanted to check out the scene in Nantes 1847, because I heard there were some fine ladies there. But I ran out of fuel in Washington DC 1969, and I've pretty much been here ever since.

Interviewer: Well, if we handed out jobs based on creativity, you'd probably score a few. Unfortunately, this is a serious job and actually, we have already filled it. But thank you for your time. You know where the door is—

Kimo: It's true and I can prove it.

Interviewer: Yeah, yeah. I've heard it all before.

Kimo: See that cup?

Interviewer: Let me guess—it's a cup from the future.

Kimo: It's your cup. What are you drinking?

Interviewer: Water.

Kimo: You're sure?

Interviewer: Yes, I just filled it. Listen, I've got—

Kimo: When I leave here today, I will go back in time to right before this meeting and I will fill your cup with coffee, so that right now you are drinking Sanka.

Interviewer: I'm telling you—hey, what the…this is coffee! Wait. You're not joking.

Kimo: No.

Interviewer: So...you could really visit the future? You can tell me what happens?

Kimo: Of course. Whatever you want to know.

Interviewer: Like how stocks will do, or where I should invest in real estate? Or who wins the next season of *The Apprentice*?

Kimo: Oh, I don't really pay attention to that stuff.

Interviewer: Well, could I go? I mean, through time. Could I time travel?

Kimo: As long as you've got the wheels.

Interviewer: You...you have wheels? Could you take me?

Kimo: Sure, that'd be totally fine. I mean, just as long as you promise not to change anything there.

Interviewer: Well, how would I even know if I was changing the future if I don't know how the future turns out?

Kimo: Huh. Good point. You're the first person to ever ask that. But on the steering wheel of every Filby, there's this warning that says you can't change history. I guess if you change history, you totally void the warranty. You're also not supposed to drive faster than so many years per minute and you're supposed to change the oil every three-thousand years. It's just like on the fuel tank where it says no fruit-on-the-bottom type yogurts.

Interviewer: Maybe the changing history thing only applies if you're going to the past?

Kimo: Maybe. But I'd still think you should be careful if you're visiting the future. I mean, dude. The warranty.

Interviewer: And you'd give me a ride? I could visit New York in 2100 or Paris in 2450. Or even someplace in the past, like Rome in 766 A.D.?

Kimo: Sure, man. But those places are like so last year. If you really want to see the future, you should check out places like Natrona 2791 or Rosebery the middle of next week. Though I've never been to Rosebery, so I can't really speak for it.

Interviewer: Well, Mr. Levernson. This is an offer. Do you

want the job?

Kimo: I'm sorry?

Interviewer: The job. That's why you're here, right? For the associate executive managing director position with the Gore/Lieberman campaign.

Kimo: But you just said the position was filled.

Interviewer: Well, now that I think about it, a position may have just opened up. Yes, Billy Thornton won't be needing his computer anymore.

Kimo: Don't you want to know about my qualifications?

Interviewer: Oh, uh, sure. Tell me your qualifications.

Kimo: Well, I ran my own summer painting business when I was in college. I actually didn't make any money, though, after I had to pay my crew. So that was kind of a scam. Oh, and I worked for three summers at the Dip n' Go, but they didn't hire me back after that, so I was unemployed for a few years. Since arriving here in 1969, I've mostly done freelance stuff. You know, mowing a lawn here, raking some leaves there, chop down a tree over there. That sort of thing.

Interviewer: Okay, great. So?

Kimo: Excuse me?

Interviewer: Great. Do you want the job?

Kimo: Um, Yeah. That sounds cool. When do I start?

Interviewer: So I'll just go talk to Billy—you wait right here —and then I can show you to your cubicle. And then after that, we can go for a ride, right?

Kimo: Sure thing.

Interviewer: Just one sec. Be right back. (Interviewer leaves.)

Kimo: I just better remember to go back and fill his cup after
I leave. Although, now that I think about it, I obviously
won't forget. Because there it is.

.   .   .

There's more. Between me and Dick Cheney, that is.

I'm writing a novel about Dick Cheney and I do
genealogy research. So of course I was curious if I could find
a connection. Maybe we aren't really blood brothers. But are
we family?

Turns out that Cheney's ninth great-grandparents were
Percival and Rebecca Lowell. And my eleventh great-
grandparents? The same Percival and Rebecca.

Hmmm...Ninth and Eleventh great-grandparents. Nine...
eleven. 9-11.

Emergency? Conspiracy?

.   .   .

Percival and Rebecca's daughter Joanna was Cheney's
eighth-great-grandmother and my tenth-great-grandmother.
But we have different grandfathers. My tenth-great-grand-
father was Joanna Lowell's first husband John Oliver, while
Cheney's eighth great-grandfather was her second husband
Captain William Gerrish. That makes me and the big guy
ninth cousins, twice removed.*

---

* *Editor's note:* For those confused by the above, we have documented the
genealogical connection between the author and Dick Cheney in the
bonus features at the novel's conclusion. See page 214.

So, yeah. If you haven't started on your way back to the 2790's, call me, Dick. Let's do lunch. We have a lot to catch up on.

.   .   .

Okay, okay—you're right. This actually makes us merely *half*-ninth cousins, twice removed. So I guess we don't have much in common after all.

Nevermind.

.   .   .

"Come on, Rummy. You've got to let me take your Filby. The Natrona prom is next weekend and I have to be there. Puh-lease!"

"You can't fool me with your arguments, Dick. Prom next week? *Everything* is next week. And tomorrow and last Tuesday. Everything is all the time when you can travel through time with a brand new state of the art Filby XJ convertible with new SupaFly™ technology. Why don't you just go to prom in a few years, once you can afford your own?"

"You're right—I could go anytime. But my anniversary is this week. When she came to live with me in 1973, Lynne gave up her senior prom. And I totally promised her I'd take her for our anniversary. We've been planning for this day for months!"

"And you've only just now thought of securing

transportation? Isn't that a little short-sighted, Dick?"

"Come on. Do you have plans or something?"

"Okay, fine. I'm just dicking you around, Dick. Of course you can go, but on one condition."

"You name it. Anything."

"You have to vote against extending the Civil Rights Act."

"You're opposed to civil rights?"

"Do you want the car or not?"

"Yeah, I want the car. But geez, man. If I had a dollar for every time I had to vote against something just so I could borrow your car. First it was cleaning up hazardous waste, then the release of Nelson Mandela from his jail cell, funding for the Veterans Administration—actually, you had me vote against that one a few times. And remember when you had me oppose the Clean Water Drinking Act?"

"I remember, Dick."

"There were like only twenty other House reps against that one. That was kind of lonely. You don't think this Civil Rights Act thing will be like that at all, do you?"

"It could be. But hey, if it's not worth it to you to take Lynne to the prom. I mean, it is only your anniversary—"

"Sorry, sorry. Okay, fine. I'll vote against the Civil Rights Act."

"Thataboy. Just make sure you have the car back by midnight."

"Of course, Rummy. Hey—maybe we could double-date! After all, you've never been to one of our earthling dances. Perhaps you could report on it to your people, so they understand some of our world's mating rituals."

"Nah—Joyce isn't really into that kind of thing. And I'd love to go myself, but I'd just be a fifth wheel, as I believe your people say."

"Uh, something like that."

"But you know, Dick. I would like to take a ride with you through time sometime. Get a better understanding of the significance of various events in your world's history. I've been reading these books and I'm unclear as to why certain things are more important than others. I think your perspective would be quite helpful. Plus, it would be great to be able to spend some quality time with you, so I can better understand what humans do when there are no witnesses—er, observers. That's what I mean."

"That sounds cool. You mean we'd pretty much go cruising through history, maybe bring along a case or two?"

"Precisely."

"Well, what are you doing right now?"

"I have to report back to my mother ship in forty-five minutes, but I think we could squeeze it in before then."

"Cool. Oh, and hey—maybe you could show me again how to put the top down. I keep messing up. And I want to be pretty suave for the anniversary prom thing."

Wanting to make sure he didn't miss his report-back, Rummy just drove Dick to the Civil War, and asked Dick a few questions. Dick didn't miss the opportunity to share his knowledge.

"Abraham Lincoln was a very brave man, I can tell you that."

Later, Rummy dropped Dick at his front door.

"Hey, Rummy. This has been awesome. We should definitely do this more often—maybe even make it a long weekend—three or four days. Then we could really go far."

"Well, Dick. What about making it an annual trip? Every year, perhaps I could take off from Searle and you could get away from Congress for the better part of a week. Just the two of us joyriding through time and drinking beer. Even keep it secret from our wives."

"What will we tell them—what if they're suspicious?"

"We could tell them something outlandish and ridiculous. Say we're developing a super-secret classified program designed to set aside the proper and traditional line of succession for the president."

"That's hilarious, Rummy. I love it."

"They wouldn't ask any more questions after that, would they?"

.   .   .

When I was a kid, one of my favorite book series was called *Time Machine*. It was sort of like those Choose-Your-Own-Adventure books, but the focus was time travel, as opposed to the whole "If you surrender to the pirates, turn to page 43. If you stand and fight the pirates, turn to page 97."

In time travel philosophy, one of the great paradoxes is known as the grandfather paradox. But times change, so let's call it the grandmother paradox.

It goes something like this: Suppose a ~~man~~ person

traveled back in time and killed his or her biological great-great-great-great-great-great-great-great-great grandfather before he met the traveler's great-great-great-great-great-great-great-great grandmother. As a result, the time traveler would never have been conceived, which would mean he or she couldn't have traveled back in time in the first place. Which means the great-great-great-great-great-great-great-great grandfather would still be alive. Which would mean the traveler would be conceived. Allowing him or her to travel back in time to kill...oh, you get the point.

So my question: If Dick Cheney traveled backward from 2792, could he keep *me* from being born? Want a taste of those *Time Machine* books? Here you go:

> If you think Dick Cheney travels back in time and kills his great-great-great-great-great-great-great-great-great grandfather, Percival Lowell, before Percy and Rebecca get it on, thereby ensuring their great-great-great-great-great-great-great-great-great-great-great grandson (me) is never born, further ensuring that this book is never written and is therefore not released the same day as Cheney's memoir (because presumably Dick Cheney also would never have been born), turn to page 195.

> If you think Cheney is unable to alter the course of this author's writing life, keep reading.

. . .

Hey, what's this?

Oh, some article about the whole Lieberman robot thing. It's quite interesting.

What Lieberman robot?

I don't know—when I'm finished, you can read the article.

Let me see that...You idiot! This is us!

Oh. I thought it sounded familiar.

I am Dr. Lieberman! I make robots! And this, this looks like a call from the past! Obviously someone is trying to get a message to us and they chose to put the message in a time capsule! We must do something about this. This is my chance to stop Al Gore from becoming president! Just think—I will be a hero of the people! I will be responsible for stopping all the pain and suffering in the world. Me, Dr. Joseph Lieberman.

But how?

That's what I still need to work out. Think, think. Perhaps if I...no, too risky.

In the article, it says you created a robot and sent it back to infiltrate Gore's campaign.

I've got it. I will create a robot.

I just said that.

Yes, but I will create a *Republican* robot that tells everyone he is a Democrat—ha ha!—until he is even believed by the Democrat Party elite. And in a time in our nation's history when all parties are doing whatever they can to move closer to the center, in order to steal votes from the other side, they will deem him the only viable choice for vice president.

But why a robot, sir? Why not just send a man?

You fool! Only a robot can parrot the same line over and over with such conviction. What if we sent a real person and he was offered money or free airline flights, or perhaps hookers or worse, a young male page? Why, a real senator would cave under that kind of pressure. He would tell his innermost dreams in exchange for a twenty-dollar steak dinner. But not a robot. Robots do not eat steak, nor do they care much for young boys. Furthermore, if we send a Republican to infiltrate the team, we definitely need his secret Republicanism to remain just that—secret. And that means no man. No. A robot must be sent. Who was it that said all it takes for evil to triumph is for good time-traveling robot-producing scientists to do nothing?

I guess I still don't understand. Why is it that we would send a Republican robot to join the Democrat party? Why not a Democrat robot?

Because! Then even if the Democrats win, they lose! Regardless of who wins the election, there will be a Republican in charge! Bwah-ha-HA! HA-ha-ha!

Um—that doesn't seem to be what the article is about, though. If you're the one they're talking about here, shouldn't you do what it says here?

Two answers: First of all, free will, my boy. There is no preordained action I am supposed to take. And I can prove it. I will do what I want and send this robot to the past, and only *then* will this article be written. And only then will I learn that I must send a robot to the past. Wait—I'm not sure this makes sense. Let me think about this a second.

Okay, doctor. I'm still not sure I get it. But what's the second answer?

Don't believe everything you read in the newspaper, my boy.

.   .   .

March 23, 2198
Los Angeles Time-Chronicle

CLEARWATER (AP) A time capsule opening at A.E. Truplinksy Middle School turned surreal yesterday, when the children found what appears to be the original letter requesting an evil robot be sent to infiltrate the Democratic Party in the late 1900s.

Historians immediately questioned its authenticity, but Retrex-dating™ has pinpointed the placement of the ink on the paper to mid-March 1998.

Principal Scuder read the letter aloud, which requested a robot be sent back in time to join the Democratic Party.

The evil robot was designed by Dr. Joseph Lieberman of Perfect Robotics Inc., a Sunnyvale company known for their popular line of synthetic replacement children for parents who have lost their kids to painful diseases. Approximately 40 years from now, Dr. Lieberman will send the robot back in time, at the 1998 request of Halliburton CEO Dick Cheney.

It wasn't revealed that Lieberman was a robot until late in the campaign, when Republicans launched what they hoped would be the "October surprise" that would turn the election against Lieberman's running mate, Al Gore.

But the robot Lieberman proved an aid to the Gore campaign, as dissatisfied voters felt the robot Lieberman gave the ticket some personality that was fore-to-then lacking.

Though Gore later took credit for the diversity of his staff, including the first robot Vice President, pundits believed Gore was originally unaware he had selected a robot running mate.

"We always knew the letter was in there," said Scuder, adding that their custodian Gus was a big student of history and had studied the Gore presidency.

"I've read lots of books on this," said Gus. "And so I knew that Cheney left a note in this time capsule in 1998 that we would open here in 2198, and which Dr. Lieberman would read about in your LA Time-Chronicle article, prompting him to work on it for years and finally get around in 2236 to sending one of his robots to 1998. So it was just a matter of time before we opened it."

"Still," added Principal Scuder. "It's pretty exciting for the kids. Now they are a part of history!"

The letter will be on display at the middle school's trophy case for the next three weeks before moving to a permanent home at the Clearwater County Historical Museum.

.   .   .

In the present, you will generally not find tourists from the future.

Steven Hawking has postulated this as an argument against the possibility of time travel. After all, if, in the year 2000, there is no one coming from 3000 or 8000 or even the year 1234567, then it must be assumed that they haven't figured out time travel by any of those years.

But this ignores an important fact: We do not believe people who say they are tourists from the future. Rather, we call the police and we lock them away.

And yet, the truth remains: tourists from the future live among us. In fact, it has been estimated that as many as ten or fifteen percent of the people we meet are tourists from the future, though you would never know from looking at them.

These tourists have learned to say they are visiting from Europe, and to not say they are from the future. Because it's not exactly a fun vacation when you're tossed in a mental institution. Which is the main reason they buy time travel insurance before they leave home. Just in case.

Worse, it is often very difficult for these individuals to find comfort and relax in our time, as our world is not designed for tourists from the future. Nor for tourists from the past, for that matter. Though I should note that tourists from the past are far less likely to visit, as it is pretty much assumed that no one from the past has the technology to travel to the future.

Mostly our world is designed for the tourist of the present. This leads to a "present assumption," in which we assume everyone we interact with is from the present, completely ignoring the possibility that they might be from a different time.

Tourists from the future are forced to live their lives as a lie, pretending to be having fun enjoying a jaunt *over to* Palm Beach, say, when in fact it is a jaunt *back to* Palm Beach.

Much worse, however, is that tourists from the future do not have the same rights as people who live in the present. For example, if a tourist from the future gets hurt in the present, their insurance will not cover them. Present hospitals are considered out-of-network. The tourist from the future must return to the future in order to receive care, or may have to pay out of pocket.

Furthermore, if the tourist from the future becomes incapacitated, their previous-of-kin are not legally able to make decisions for them, such as whether to have certain medical procedures performed. It can be left to the state to make decisions, despite the fact that they may have distant ancestors perfectly capable of making those decisions.

So if you meet someone and he or she confides in you that he or she is a tourist from the future, please show some compassion and support. It may seem exotic to you, but know that they face numerous challenges on a daily basis.

.　　.　　.

Several years ago, I worked for an on-demand publishing company. If you're not familiar with "on-demand," the concept is that DVDs and books are made only when there is an order for them. That way, there's no need for struggling artists to buy a huge inventory that might take a garage to store and forever to sell.

In testing the book program, one day I uploaded my *Dick Cheney Saves Paris* file and ordered a copy. I did the same for two other books. I wasn't planning on self-publishing these books, but since it was really just a one-time printing for myself, I figured what the heck. I mean, it's not like printing one book for myself could stop me from finding a publisher some day, right? Plus, I was paid to test the system. So I tried it out.

But did I mention that Amazon.com had bought the company? And that when I tested out the book process, there was a bug that allowed my books to be listed on their website? Yes, you could see a detail page for *Dick Cheney Saves Paris* with the very simple cover I tossed on it.

I let the tech people know and they fixed the bug. The books were never actually for sale, as I hadn't approved the proofs for them, so there was no chance of someone buying a copy. I was told the books would no longer show up on the website. A few weeks later I checked, just to confirm.

Lo and behold, one of the three was still there.

.   .   .

From the Journal of Dick Cheney

August 10, 1995

Held a news conference today at Halliburton HQ to tell the world I'll be the CEO until further notice. I gave them some bullshit line about wrapping up my political career. What did I say? Oh, yeah: 'When I made the decision earlier this year not to run for president, not to seek the White House, that really was a decision to wrap up my political career and move on to other things.'

But after 26 years in this game, I'm not going anywhere. I still have 5 years before I can be sure Al Gore is not elected. In the meantime, I'm just trying to get my hands on some moolah to dish on the political machine—grease some wheels.

October 23, 1995

Been thinking lately about my legacy and what history will say about me once I save the world from Al Gore. I know future generations will have their own interpretations of my actions, but I think it's important that they get my side, too. Sure, there will be my journals that will probably be published after I die, or perhaps they'll just end up at some presidential library. But then I won't be able to profit off my story. And that would be un-American, so that would never do.

Therefore I've decided to write my autobiography. At this point all I have is the title, but I'm pretty sure I know how it would begin, so maybe I'll toy with it here, see how it comes out...

Captain Dick Saves the World:
The Future Journal of Dick Cheney
By Richard Bruce "Dick" Cheney

They say a story is of interest to all for two reasons: either it is extraordinary and anyone will want to read about; or it is universal and everyone can relate to the tale of the ordinary everyday everyman. Well, this is the story of the extraordinary everyman. The person going about his day, doing his thing, just trying to get by, but who somehow manages to alter the course. Of history.

I'm Dick Cheney. And this is my story.

I was born January 30, 2754 to Richard and Marjorie Cheney, of Natrona in the U.S. state of Stebold. Our life was not easy, but through dedication, motivation, tenacity, lots of hard work, and a little bit of luck, we were able to pull ourselves up from a dreary middle lower middle class existence to a comfortable upper lower middle class lifestyle.

School was easy for me. From an early age, I was particularly good at transmorphing the elements of my studies into my internal kimptomatter patch. Naturally straight A's followed, and I was soon racing through Yale in pursuit of something larger than myself.

Somewhere on the way to something larger than myself, however, I fell into a hard-charging party like it's 2799 lifestyle. The world was my oyster, and I cracked it open and added warm butter and some spinach. Life was a bowl of cherries and I made lemonade out of it. I drank the Kool-Aid.

However, let this be a warning to all young people. Do not read this as me saying it's okay to blow off school and party your life away. You must first get a college degree. And then you can party. I found out the hard way—by doing—but you can learn from my experience: If you have a degree, party as much as you want. Because if you have that degree to fall back on, no matter what a pathetic blob you are, you are still at least one step ahead of the average skilled, intelligent, hard-working person who can not afford a college degree.

When I was 27, I got my life back on track and put my partying days behind me. I had the opportunity to travel. A friend was going to Nantes, 1847 to study the role of women in society, and he suggested I come along. "Sure," I said. "But only if we first stop off in Washington, D.C., circa 1969."

"Why would you want to do that, Dick?" he asked.

"Because," I said. "Only then can I dedicate my life to saving the world from the presidency of Al Gore."

"I don't know," said Kimo. "It sounds dangerous."

"Dangerous is my middle name," I said.

"I thought your middle name was Bruce," said Kimo.

"No. It may have been in the past. But from this day forward, let all know that I shall be called 'Richard Danger "Dick" Cheney.'"

"I can still call you 'Dick,' right?"

"Of course," I said. "I'll still go by my nickname."

Wow—so far, so good! I know I'm not a captain or anything, but I thought it added a little "I don't know what." I especially like the idea of sharing lessons on life with young people, like the fact that you can party all you want if you have a college degree. In addition to a memoir, it can also be a self-help book. I should probably throw in something about honesty and integrity. Maybe say something about chopping down an apple tree in my youth.

I'll have to keep working on it in my spare time. But what I have so far should be enough to find me a publisher. Heck, I bet I can get a bidding war out of this and end up with a 9-figure advance. But more important than the money is that *I* will be the one to make up the details—how I convinced Kimo to stop off in 1969, the time I stood up Katie Driscoll for prom, hot romances with celebrities, that sort of thing.

Yes, I will get to decide what my story is—not some asshole historian or goddamn ghostwriter. You just can't leave important stuff like this to other people. They get bogged down in the facts.

November 1, 1996

Been hanging out with Rummy again. I really miss the old days. It would be so great if we could get the old guys back together again. Me, Rummy, Wolfowitz, Steve Forbes, Doug Feith, Gary Bauer, Elliot Abrams, and Billy Kristol, heck—even Scooter Libby. They've all scattered to their lives: getting married, buying homes, having kids, becoming CEOs of multi-national corporations, making car payments, and so on.

Maybe we could develop some kind of weekly activity— like a bowling night or card night. Get together, drink a few beers, relive the old times.

December 13, 1996

I talked to Rummy about my card night idea and he said he had a better idea. I asked what could be better than playing cards? He said that's exactly what we'd be doing—playing cards—but since we are all thinking about our cards, and we are all leaders, we should call it a think tank with a self-stated goal to promote American global leadership. He also said it would help keep an air of mystery about ourselves. Plus, he said, if we told our wives we had to get to our think tank, it might go over better than, "Hey, hon. I'm going to Rummy's to play poker and down some bourbon." Honestly, I think Lynne wouldn't care one way or the other, so I think he's the one who might have the problem—perhaps he has to tiptoe around Joyce a little.

We're going to start after the first of the year—after the holidays. I'm psyched.

January 10, 1997

Today was our second week of cards. It's really cool. All the gang is there. I just wish Kimo could see me now.

Wolfowitz came up with a name for our little group. Rummy's favorite card game is pinochle (I'm partial to Hearts but Rummy can be a little aggressive if you know what I'm saying, so we usually end up doing what he wants), and when he was trying to think of a good secret acronym for our group —something like NSA, Perle said "You like pinochle so much, why not call it P-NUC?"

Rummy liked it and was trying to think up what it could stand for if we were pressed by our wives. He was like, "Huh, Professional National...People's National...Union...Political National Union. No. Hmph."

And then Wolf goes, "I've got it. Project for the New American Century." Rummy just smiled.

I know that's PNAC, not PNUC, but we all thought it was close enough. So now we have our think tank to promote America in the world—though really we'll just be playing cards.

Please, dear diary, don't tell Lynne. She'll think it's "just plain silly."

.　.　.

Apple pie landed with a thud at the side of the road. She watched the Filby continue slowing. It was going so fast when she jumped, that by the time the car rolled to a stop, it was out of view.

Good, she thought. I've got at least a few years on them.

She started walking and soon came upon Washington, DC 1998.

Well, she thought. I'm much closer than I expected.

In town, she quickly ditched her cardboard sign and grabbed a double cappuccino at the White House gift store. It was a long trip and she needed the extra boost. Besides, they don't make doubles anymore. In the future, it's all quintuple and sextuple cappuccinos and she was curious to give it a try

Hmmm, she thought. Should I get a gift for Weena now, or wait until I'm done with everything? Perhaps a little window-shopping will help.

But then, she realized she'd never seen the Washington Monument, the Lincoln Memorial, or the Lieberman Monument, all of which were exploded during World War VI, when the U.S. wanted to pin something on the Canadians. And heck, the election she needed to affect was over two years away, anyway. She could take the time to do a little touring about, what would it hurt? Gore would still be there when she finished.

Plus, if she did miss something she should have been working on, perhaps she could go hitchhiking again. She didn't have any trouble being picked up that last time—she was only out on the road for a few minutes when the car stopped.

Yes, it was decided. She would check out the DC scene. Probably not all the museums of the Smithsonian. Though it would probably be helpful to see as much as she could, if only to advance her understanding of American history, for whatever assignment she received next.

Huh, she thought. It's funny being a tourist from the future. Especially if she could take all the time she wanted to relax in her hotel and then go back a week and do it again.

Hmmm, maybe these 1990's won't be so bad after all.

Her first stop was the McDonald's near Michigan and Seventh.

Can I please have the number four? she asked. The chicken nugget meal. And a Diet Coke.

Would you like to supersize it?

What? Oh, no thank you. She had learned about this option of the past, but was caught off guard, as the article in the recent Journal of Historical Fast Food had called it *upsizing*. The woman behind the counter should have said, Would you like to upsize? She made a mental note to write a letter to the editor. It was bad information like this that could cost her a job.

She handed over the four dollars and twelve cents and accepted the tray. Oh, she said, could I have an extra barbecue? She was keen to try out this line.

Sure, said the cashier, before handing her two packets. Success!

Then she grabbed her tray, turned around, and almost walked right into Dick Cheney.

Well, hello, he said.

. . .

In the future, man can intentionally destroy some aspect of society, but only every six years.

It's a very serious matter, with some groups even opposed to changing history in any way whatsoever. Because once something is gone—it's gone. It's not like you can completely eradicate the plague of 1912 and then decide in 2654 you want it back. Well, okay, bad example—they actually did bring it back in 2654. It was picked in 2648, someone went back and destroyed it and then six years later, with the campaign strength of the People Ordinarily Opposed to Changing History (POOCH), they voted to eliminate the guy who went back in 2648—before he was born. Meaning of course, that he could never go back in 2648 to 1912.

That was a tough time for that guy. Yes, he had returned to 2648 after successfully eradicating the plague. And he thought he would return a hero. But the 2648 he came back to was quite a different place than the 2648 he left. And so he was around 6 years later when POOCH ran their campaign, and he fearfully watched their popularity surge higher and higher as the vote approached.

Vreebul Daily Star
November 3, 2654

Dear Editor:
I strongly urge all citizens to vote against eradicating me from the earth. It doesn't even make sense if you think about it.

Besides, my mission is now part of history, so these so-called People Opposed to Changing History are complete hypocrites if they are trying to change my historical changing of history. Hell—if they want it changed, why not just eradicate the 2648 vote!

Why does it have to be me? Why not eradicate Stephen Urtley, the man who at the U.N. History Altering Council first proposed adding the 1912 Plague to the vote. I strongly urge anyone who wants to hold a person responsible to write-in Stephen Urtley's name. I was just doing a job.

On November 6, please don't shoot the messenger.

Sincerely,
Turl Bignuth, FRM Agent #34009
United Nations Dept. of Undoing History, Neatly
(UN-DUHN)

Sure, there are always those activist groups who manage to get enough signatures and put completely essential things on the ballot—like oxygen or water or even yogurt. Trying to prove some point or other that we shouldn't leave it to the people to decide such important matters.

Others use the vote to register their political beliefs: some want Jesus Christ eradicated or some pope or other. But people are generally too smart to fall for their marketing campaigns, and they never muster more than a percentage or so of the vote. ("Religion" being an exception when it received 23% of the vote in 2336.)

No, generally it's things that have ruined civilizations or appear to be heading toward destruction of a civilization.

Sometimes it is even a person—or more accurately, the philosophy of a person. But it could be just about anything. In 2348, it was neo-Naziism. In 2472, yoga. In 2502, Mitch Albom's entire milieu, including *Tuesdays with Morrie*, *The Five People You Meet in Heaven*, and his last book, written during his downward spiral into depression, *Pass the Sugar, Bitch: I'm Tired of Your Fat Face.*

The closest vote ever came in 2608, when Pittsburgh Pirates second baseman Bill Mazeroski's 1960 World Series home run against the New York Yankees just barely edged out the Irish potato famine of the 1850's. The potato famine never recovered and has been dipping in popularity ever since. Sporting events, however, have been on the rise, but they rarely get enough support to win the vote. Fans from opposing sides usually end up splitting the vote, making the Mazeroski vote that much more surprising (though perhaps there are more Yankees fans than Pirates fans).

The man chosen to make sure Bill Mazeroski was taken out had a very different reception from Turl Bignuth. Upon his return, UN-DUHN agent Shep Nirtley received a ticker-tape parade in his honor.

. . .

I thought of complaining about my book appearing on Amazon.com, but I kind of liked the idea that people doing a search for "Dick Cheney" on Amazon.com might stumble across this:

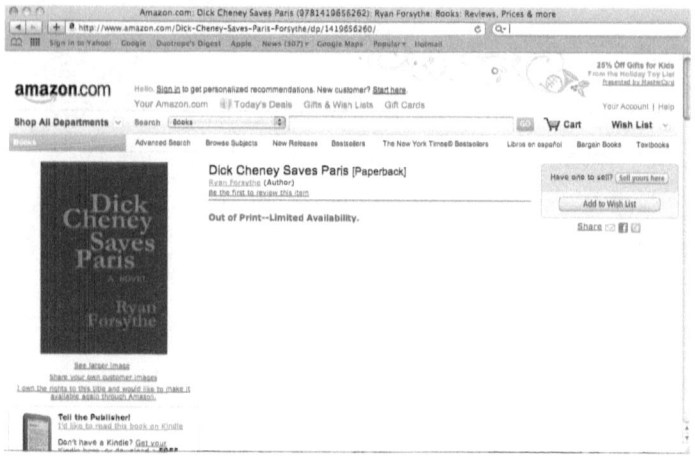

My only concern was if and when I did submit the novel to a publisher, maybe this would stop it from being picked up: the fact that it *looks* like it has already been self-published.

Sure, it says "Out of Print—Limited Availability." I had the only copy, after all. But despite what the world's largest bookseller would have you believe, I swear there was never any availability. Just one copy, printed for my own bookshelf.

Until now, that is. The people at Love Earth Publications liked the book enough to make several more of the revised and expanded edition.

Perhaps you're even reading one this very minute.

. . .

"Apple pie. So, we meet again."

"How...how did you get here? I thought I had a big head

start on you."

"Well, where did you land when you jumped from the Filby?"

"1998."

"Ninety-eight? It looks like you did have a head start on me. Would you believe I ended up stuck in 1969. But time marches on. And so here we both are in 1998."

"Yes."

"Something tells me it was not an accident that we picked you up that day. You knew Hillyer?"

"Yes. I knew him. He hired me. But I didn't know he would be there. I was honestly trying to get to Des Moines. I want to be settled in and ready by the time the primaries roll around. And then, there he was in the back seat."

"And you don't know what he's up to?"

"Listen. I was hired by Hillyer to stop Gore. So all I can assume is that either he was checking up on me, or checking up on you. I don't know."

"Sounds like we have a lot in common. It's my goal to stop Gore. It's your goal to stop Gore. You wouldn't consider forming a...partnership?"

"Sorry, Dick."

"Well, that's too bad. Trust issues?"

"Something like that, yes. My employer has reason for me to stop Gore before anyone else. There's a lot at stake. So this is something that I must do alone."

"I imagine we will meet again sometime before the election is over. I do wish you luck, Apple pie. If either of us can stop Gore, then it will mean the end of all pain and suffering in the world."

"I can't really wish you luck, Dick. But good luck to you. May the best person win."

As Apple pie walked out, Rummy walked in.

"Who was that?"

"Oh, no one. Just some woman I met."

"You're not..."

"I'm not what?"

"You know...with...you know?"

"Rummy, I have no idea what you're talking about."

"Cheating, dammit Are you cheating?"

"What? Oh, no, no. No. I could never cheat on Lynne. No, that was just someone who had similar interests as me, as pertains to stopping Al Gore. I tell you, Rummy. I'm beginning to suspect that this is going to be a lot harder than initially thought."

"Are you *still* on that whole stop Al Gore kick? God, I thought you were over that by now. It's been decades."

"Can I help who's next?"

"I'm just getting warmed up, Rummy. The time is almost at hand. Gore will be announcing his intent to run for president any day now. I need to somehow slow his momentum—keep him from gaining critical mass. Unfortunately, I don't think any of my efforts to date have had an impact on the outcome."

"I know. I was just over to 2012—visiting my good friend the chief justice to help a distant cousin with its—er, with *his* political campaign—and noticed that Gore wins not only in 2000, but he's re-elected in a landslide in 2004. And to top it off, his V.P. Shecky Cornhiser wins in 2008. The immediate future doesn't look so good for the Republican party."

"But what more can I do?"

"Can I help who's next?"

"Well, why don't you just send a message to the future to send reinforcements."

"What reinforcements? Who is going to come stop Gore? And who would I send this message to? I mean, how would they do it anyway? What could someone from the future do that I couldn't do?"

"Maybe they'll have the technology to create a replacement Gore. And then you can take out the real one and replace him with the dummy. Then, when he wins, you'll control him!"

"But I don't want him to win. That's just it. I think even if a fake Gore wins, it may be the same result, the same effect on history. Though it's an interesting thought. If a different Gore wins, is it so bad? I guess since my dad was always talking about Al Gore's presidency, that it might not matter whether it was a real or fake—it would still be an Al Gore, right? And hell—maybe if I did replace Gore with a fake, then it's possible that the fake is the one that my dad is always pissed off about."

"Wait, that doesn't even make sense. You're saying that because your dad hates Al Gore, that perhaps you are here to change Al Gore and you may change him into the Al Gore that your dad hates? Thereby causing your dad to complain about him, and therefore prompting you to come here and change him? Again?"

"It's a concern."

"Hmmm."

"But if he was complaining about the fake Gore and I came here to change him, then would it be possible that changing him to a real Gore would cause my father no consternation? Or would I, perhaps, need to change him to a different fake?"

"I don't know."

"Can I help who's next?"

"You better step up—they seem to be getting antsy or something."

"Give me two Filet-o-Fish and a small fry."

"Would you like a beverage?"

"No. Rummy, let's just drop the whole replacing Al Gore thing. Assuming no Al Gore wins, I think we can safely assume my father won't complain about any Al Gore, real or fake. But you may be on to something with the synthetic person from the future angle. Let me think about this."

"Just don't think too long."

"That'll be four twenty-nine."

"I've got it!"

"Wow. That wasn't long. What are you going to do?"

"Let's just say Shecky Cornhiser doesn't strike me as much of a vice presidential name."

"Here's your change, sir. Seventy-one cents. Can I help you, sir?"

"Yes. Gimme one of those Shamrock shakes. You're going to change *their* guy? How the hell are you going to do that?"

.　.　.

By the way, I'm not sure how Amazon.com determines the categories for their books. On the webpage noted above, *Dick Cheney Saves Paris* ended up listed under "Literature & Fiction," "Nonfiction > Philosophy," and also "Religion & Spirituality > Religious Studies > Science & Religion."

With this whole thing I'm doing, I can see the nonfiction and maybe even the philosophy and science parts. But that version had none of this. Nowhere in the 2006 version did I talk about Miss Snark or finding out about Dick Cheney's memoir in 2011 or even about making a Syria travel brochure in sixth grade and watching the Iran-Contra affair a summer or two later. It was straight fiction.

I have another book on Amazon that has a strange category. *The Little Veal Cutlet That Couldn't* is listed under "Health, Mind & Body > Diets & Weight Loss > Diets." I get the "Health" connection considering it was a children's book (for adults) showing the abuse of cows in making veal. And I guess for those kids who run screaming from veal after seeing the illustrations, it might lead to some weight loss.

So maybe "diet" is the perfect category.

.　.　.

This has been really nice, honey.

I agree. When was the last time we took a trip, just you and me, no kids?

I don't know—I think it was that trip back to Niagara

Falls before they dried up in the 23rd century.

Didn't Mandy come with us then?

Oh, that's right. Randy was camping with the Brugersons. Wasn't Mandy upset about something? Maybe one of her rabbits had died. That would make our last time alone sometime before Mandy was born. Wow. Thank god Shirley could watch the kids on such short notice.

Well, she does owe us one for all the times we watched her kids when she and Rod would go swinging through the Mediterranean at the turns of the centuries.

Hey—can you pull over at the next stop. I really need to pee.

Didn't you just go?

No, that was over three centuries ago.

Honey, at the speed we're going, that was twenty-five minutes ago. Can't you hold it? We're almost to 2000.

What are you talking about? We won't be to 2000 for at least ten minutes. Pull over.

The sign said there were fairly limited services at this exit. Can you hold it until the next one? I'm pretty sure there's an IHOP at the next stop. You know how they have them at every other exit.

I need to go. And you are not eating any more pancakes.

Plus, we'll need to fill up soon. The exit after this one has a station.

Darling, pull over. I promise you can still fill up at the next exit.

Okay, I'm pulling off. But please tell me where you want me to stop. Like I said, there aren't any services.

Well, where are we?

I think this is Palestine 2142. Though the guns that man has makes me think it's closer to Haifa 2135.

Oh, Harold. I don't think we should have stopped here. Let's keep going. Please get back on the Interyear.

What? You made me get off here and you want to keep going?

Yes. Don't stop here.

If you need to go, then go. I'm sure we'll be fine.

Harold.

I won't say I told you so—

You didn't tell me the exit was a war zone.

But I told you so.

If it makes you happy, we can stop at the IHOP. I'll use their bathroom.

Alright. Next stop, the Interannual House of Pancakes. But that's the last stop before Gore's inauguration.

.   .   .

In the past, time travel to the future was seen as something glamorous. In reality, time travel is both dirty and dangerous.

When the yogurt gets properly warmed and the kficvabt is running most efficiently, the carbon dioxide funnels into the driver compartment. People tend to believe that since regular (non time-travel) automobiles funnel the wastes out into the environment, that time machines would do the same. But this would go against one of the principle laws of time travel, to not alter history. This law was first explicitly stated in the U.N. Budapest Convention of 2341 in Section 4, item a.7.4-b: "The individual time traveler should, under no circumstance, alter the actual events or appearance of said events, due to the time traveler's presence and/or lack thereof." Naturally, this led to much discussion of what 'should' means, whether it is a specific mandate or more of a suggestion.

Though the "law" may be debated, it is clear that history is slowly being diminished. The leading cause is assumed to be time machine emissions. However, there are plenty of scientists who have come down on the side that emissions particles have no effect on history. They argue that history has always ebbed and flowed—that in the age of dinosaurs, history was slowly being diminished, for example, but that history came back strong, and we should have no reason to doubt that it will again.

But increasingly, a rich body of research seems to firmly indicate that history is being degraded a little at a time, and time machine emissions are the main culprit. Recent estimates indicate that by the year 14920, history will become extinct. The irony is that the very act of visiting history is the leading cause of the degradation of history.

At first, the UN asked the time machine makers to voluntarily implement stricter emissions controls. But companies such as Filby and Yleuro did nothing. Then the UN mandated the policies. The companies stated that it would hurt the bottom line—thousands of people would have to be laid off and they would have to move their factories to the 18th and 19th centuries in order to stay competitive.

Eventually, Druylk took the lead in creating a zero emissions time machine. Their brain trust realized that there had to be an answer to the emissions problem, and they tried to look outside the box. Just about every idea they had was inefficient or overly expensive. Nothing worked. Finally, they found the solution. And it was fairly easy to implement: funneling the emissions back into the driver compartment. The driver breathed in the emissions and the vehicle released nothing into the air. It was a brilliant method for creating a zero emissions vehicle without having to drastically alter the chief design concept.

When Filby and Yleuro caught wind of Druylk's idea, they copied the concept. The end result is no jobs were lost and no factories were sent over centuries.

However, the U.N. sued the Big Three time machine makers when several time machine drivers were found to drive with the windows rolled down completely, thereby releasing their emissions into the environment.

Now all time machines carry the government-mandated label: "Please keep driver and passenger windows rolled up completely in order to maintain zero emissions." And also: "Time machines can be dangerous to your health. Time travel may cause lung cancer, heart problems, or death. Pregnant women are encouraged to refrain from time travel."

A few people have died from the fumes, but most people ignore the laws and just keep the window cracked a tad. It's not a pull-over type offense, meaning if that's all you're doing wrong, the authorities can't pull you over. But if stopped for another reason, you can be ticketed and fined for leaking fumes into history.

.   .   .

At one point Amazon.com sponsored ads on the various book pages. Maybe they still do, I don't really know. One time I was checking the page for *The Little Veal Cutlet That Couldn't* and saw an ad for mail-order veal. Not sure if the mail-order company realized they were advertising their veal on a page presumably viewed by those pondering the purchase of a decidedly anti-veal book.

Perhaps their market research has shown that that is just the population to salivate over a picture of a veal cutlet. Who is more likely to stay away from veal at stores than food activists? Wouldn't want to be seen popping a package on the conveyer at Ralph's. So of course they would stick to mail-order.

I understand that on occasion Amazon.com has been known to de-list books they don't like (or maybe its books by people they don't like). So let the record show that I am absolutely not mocking them. Mail-order veal, yes. Amazon's category choices for some books, maybe. But certainly not Amazon.com's general je ne sais pas.

Heck, I may have even signed a non-mocking agreement when they took over that on-demand company I was working for. As I recall there were a whole bunch of papers I had to sign. So I couldn't make fun even if I wanted to. Though I may have to double-check on that and get back to you.

Though maybe I'm getting too far removed from Dick Cheney. Is the personal part of my book too personal? Not political enough? Or is the personal...political?

.   .   .

"Hello, John."

"Dick, how's it going?"

"Fine, thanks. Listen, I've got a favor to ask of you. Would you do me a favor?"

"Let's hear it first. I never promise anything until I can hear what it is."

"Shoot. I was half hoping you'd say 'Sure' and then if I told you and you didn't like the idea, I could still say 'You said you would!' and hold you to it."

McCain faked a smile. "I have to go now, Dick."

"Wait! Wait. Okay, I'll tell you. I'd like to ask you to step down in your campaign. I have reason to believe you can't win against Gore. In fact, I have a very strong reason to believe that you will get majorly thumped by Gore. To the tune of carrying only 13 states and 92 electoral votes. I mean, it's not like a Mondale type thumping, but it certainly approaches Mondale-esque proportions."

"Were you going to ask me a favor, Dick, or just stand here belittling my campaign?"

"Yes, sorry. I think it would be for the best if you concentrated on the 2004 election. I'd like to ask you to quit the race."

"Goodbye, Dick."

"Please, hear me out. It's for the good of mankind. If you don't step aside, then Al Gore will win, and he will bring about pain and suffering the nature of which our country has not seen since FDR."

"FDR brought us *out* of the depression, Dick. The New Deal? Sound familiar?"

"Yes, but trust me on this. History is constantly being rewritten. In time, he will be known as one of our worst presidents. Up there with Jefferson, Truman, Segdeyivev, and SPO-20."

"Who?"

"Oh, sorry. He must have been after your time."

"Tell Lynne I said hi."

McCain turned and walked out.

"Asshole," uttered Dick Cheney. "Damn, damn, damn. I need to find someone I can control—someone I can mold into the very model of a people's presidential candidate."

Just then, former President Bush walked by. "Oh, hi there, George. Haven't seen you in a while."

"Well, hello there, Mr. Cheney. Fancy seeing you here. I sure do remember those old days fondly, huh? Remember when we went in to Iraq—we went in swinging, yes we did. But say, I've got a favor to ask you. Let me know if I'm being forward, but could you watch my son this weekend."

"You want—you want me to babysit? But isn't your son like 45 years old?"

"Oh, I see, you want to talk money. Sure thing—I can give you $10 per hour—now I know that's more than the prevailing wage, yes I do. Wouldn't be prudent to not know the prevailing wage."

"I hear you. Say, George. Does your son entertain aspirations of someday being president?"

"Oh, I don't know if George entertains aspirations."

"Aspirations of being president, you mean?"

"Oh, no. Aspirations. Period. You know: aspirations. But I can certainly ask him, if you'd like."

"Would you? I'm trying to find a candidate to support for the primaries—"

"Well, how about that McCain feller. He seems right fine, yes he does."

"—and to whom, as CEO of Halliburton, I could give a few bijillion dollars for their campaign."

"Never liked that John McCain, no I have not. Did I say little George doesn't entertain aspirations? My bad, my very bad. I think I thought you meant something else. Ha ha. Oh, George absolutely entertains aspirations of being a presidential candidate. Just last week he said 'Dad—I wanna be president when I grow up.'"

"That's wonderful."

"And of course, I'm sure that if he's elected, he'd be more than happy to provide some, shall we say, consideration, for your company. Energy policy, if you know what I'm saying." Here, George winked, a little too obviously for Dick's taste. "That's what we Bushes are about, yes, sir. Consideration. Aspiration."

"Oh, I don't care about consideration. I'm not doing this for Halliburton. I just want to beat Gore."

"That may be true now, Mr. Cheney. But just wait until

you have connections to someone in the ol' White House. You may not realize it, but it can really change a person."

"I know all about that, George. You may recall I worked for your administration."

"Say—that's right! Well, I gotta go now, gotta go, yes I do. Say, can I drop George off at six on Friday?"

"Yes, that should be fine."

One weekend with this kid, thought Dick. And I will make him a presidential candidate. Now, to stop the McCain campaign. Hmmm. I really hate to have to do this, but I see an African-American child out of wedlock in your future, John.

.   .   .

Hello?

Hi. Is this campaign chairman Daley?

Yes, this is William Daley. Who's this?

I'm...I'm Samuel Deegan, you remember me? The new intern for Senator Lieberman?

Yes. Hi Samuel. What can I do for you? Is everything okay? Do you need more pamphlets? I'll get you more pamphlets.

Well, I don't know how to say this.

Time is money, Samuel.

Yes. Sorry, sir. It's just that… Well. Okay, I'll just say it. Senator Lieberman just lost his head, sir. And I didn't know who else to call.

Why are you wasting my time, Samuel. I have the entire

Gore campaign to deal with. If he's loopy from just winning the VP spot, give the man a sedative or a joint or something and don't call me again—

No, I mean literally. He lost his head. It came off and a few pieces disappeared under the couch. Though I think those were just some washers.

What? What are you talking about?

His head separated from his body. He seems okay—he's still talking. It's just that we're having trouble keeping his head attached.

You're making no sense, son. How is this possible?

Well, it seems the screws are stripped, sir.

No, no. I mean, how is any of this possible? If you're pulling my leg, by god I'll—

No, sir. It's the truth. It appears that he is a robot from the future, sir. And they have a very different type of screw. So that's adding to the trouble. We can't find a proper replacement.

Was he not vetted? I trusted the guys in research to vet every V.P. candidate—in great detail. I need to know everything that might come back to bite us in the ass. Leave no stone unturned. Google like mad. Did Lieberman list this future robot thing on his qualification sheet? Because if he didn't, I have half a mind to—

Um...actually he did list it. But it looks like nobody read it. It's right below his party affiliation, sir, where he wrote that he is not a Republican.

Goddammit, why do these things always happen to me? Okay, let me think. Okay. We actually don't need him to appear in public for another week. Sure, it'll hurt. We could really use his face at a few meet-n-greets. But I don't need him until Lansing. Shit. This couldn't have waited until after the debates, huh?

Sorry, sir. If there's anything I can do.

No. Let me take care of this. I've had a lot of experience cleaning up messes like this.

Thank you, sir.

. . .

You want more on Cheney? How about this: Contrary to popular convention, he pronounces his last name to rhyme with *genie*, not *zany*. But in reading this book, you can go ahead and pronounce the name however you like. Perhaps here, my completely invented character Dick Cheney pronounces his name Shay-NAY.

That said, never let an author—or one of his or her characters for that matter—tell you how to read the book.

Besides, Cheney has said, "I'll respond to either. It really doesn't matter."

. . .

In the present, no one knows what the year 4307 will bring. But they will know soon enough, because the year 4307 will bring dramatic change to late 2016.

By 4307, people will have developed a level of discretion regarding their time travels. In fact, it will be considered somewhat crass to time travel in public, something only vagrants do. And that's only when they can afford a nice Filby or Yleuro. Which vagrants will never be able to do. Because if they could afford it, then they would no longer be vagrants.

But late in the year 4307, a high-level top-secret U.S. military commando unit will arrive on a mission to nab a working time machine and as much information as possible about it, preferably a user manual and instructions for how to build the thing.

They will succeed and depart quickly, but not before they are noticed. When they race out of the Chouli laboratory of the time travel division of General Electric, Inc., with a General Electric Epoch Phase Transmitter 6900 XL 2.1, they will be spotted. Not by any of the lab's neighbors—they will make sure of that.

No, their act will be witnessed by something more sinister, the Jhelohsh of planet Minos X-43 (our classification; the locals refer to it as 'Shhholhohsh'). The Jhelohsh have developed the technology to travel undetected through space, and will set up stations for watching the people of the earth, in order that they may learn as much as possible about earth culture. But they will not have figured out time travel, for yogurt cultures can not grow in the harsh climate of Shhholhohsh.

The Jhelohsh can not see through walls, so they just hang around in public areas, keeping an eye on things. Yes, it will seem odd to them that sometimes someone disappears into their house and does not reappear for several weeks—times that the individuals were vacationing in other eras—but there won't be anything they can do to understand this curious human trait. So they wait and watch.

But then a few excited and careless Americans will run out of this lab, with a GE EPT9K, jump in a Filby, and take off. The Jhelohsh will see them vanish.

"Shejellosowellojoshesowejosh," one will say. *I think that was a time machine.*

Yes, these aliens will be smart enough to travel through space, and they will also be smart enough to see that what these strange beings had was a time machine. And they will be smart enough to invade the lab, kill all the people, steal all the Epoch Phase Transmitters, and go joyriding on their way to 2011.

By arriving in the distant future, the Americans will change the not-so distant future. When the Jhelohsh arrive in 2011, they will learn that—unlike 4307—the earth has not created a kzvuyoptud to generate a force field against any hostile alien spacecraft.

And so, the Jhelohsh will visit 2011 and plant their anti-kzvuyoptuds, which can render useless any later force fields. The world will not even realize that they have been left open to potential disaster.

Worse, the Jhelohsh will field their own U.S. presidential candidate. Their lawyers will argue that the Constitution may require people to be native-born citizens in order to run for president, but nowhere does it forbid non-people from serving in the nation's highest office. In a 5-4 decision just prior to the 2012 election, the U.S. Supreme Court will agree.

With little time to run a successful campaign, Shselllojo Jhelohsh will receive less than one percent of the vote. However, in the 2016 election, despite analysts believing the party had no real chance of victory, Shselllojo will win the presidency running on a campaign of "Sejollewesheso and Wejoshejel." It will be discussed ad nauseam, but the belief will be that a general distrust of earth politicians will lead to the result. Also, poor voter turnout will be cited frequently.

All due to the American government's desire to have time travel technology without working for it.

.   .   .

From the Journal of Dick Cheney

April 15, 2000

George asked me today to head the committee to pick a V.P. I was all like, of course I'd be happy to help, though I'm not interested myself, you know. He was all, of course. So then he handed over loads of sensitive material on all these people. I was like damn—look at all this great reading material. It's amazing what these people have been up to for the past several years.

And I'm really not interested in being V.P. I strongly believe that if elected, a person should serve out his term. But I have a plan: Gore loses, my work is done, time to go home. No way am I going to be sticking around this place for another four years.

So there is much work to be done.

April 16, 2000

Last night I glanced through the files. My god—isn't there one high-up politician in the Republican party who:

a) has 2/3 of a brain,

b) is not a woman or minority,

c) has no history of sleeping with pages,

d) has not killed anyone, and

e) harbors no secret gay or lesbian child to potentially cause a scene with the funders?

Is it really so much to ask to find one person who fits all of the above?

April 18, 2000

Still depressed over the state of the Republican Party today. I couldn't get out of bed, so Lynne brought me my food, but she also passed me an interesting article on the Stanford Prison experiment, in which volunteers were assigned the status of either prisoner or jailor. It got, like, way out of hand. I thought to myself, wow—that's hot. But it was also kinda quaint. I mean, it was like years ago—in the 1950s or something. And with just a handful of people. And that's when I decided to conduct my own experiment.

What if I could do the same, but on a much larger scale—say, with the population of a small middle-eastern country? And maybe transport a bunch of people to an undisclosed prison somewhere—like Cuba—and ask the "guards" to torture them. Would they do it? What if I asked them to attach wires to the genitals of these prisoners—would they do it? There was only one way to find out.

I think really what it comes down to is that I am approaching the end. For 30 years I've been working toward this moment. And finally it is within my reach—Al Gore will not become president. So then what? What meaning does life have for me once I've fulfilled my father's wish?

Now I had a new reason to go on. Al Gore will lose, but if *I* could be V.P., then at least I could play out my little prison scenario.

It'll be my gift to myself for a job well done.

.   .   .

John Nance Garner once said the office of Vice President was "not worth a bucket of warm piss." Others believe the quotation is that the office "isn't worth a pitcher of warm piss."

Regardless, he should know. Garner was FDR's first vice president.

.   .   .

Hey John, what are you doing here?

Well, John, I'm not supposed to say—I'm on assignment.

Me, too. Hey—I'll tell you mine if you tell me yours.

You go first.

I'm here to stop Gore from winning the election. What about you?

Oh, I've been selected to stop Bush from winning in 2004. I kinda figured if I could stop him from winning 2000, then I'd be stopping him from winning 2004, as well. You know how they do that.

Now, wait a minute, John. If you're trying to get Bush not elected and I'm trying to get Gore not elected, then I think you're working against me. Why didn't you just go to 2004 in the first place?

I know, John. I just—it's just that if he wins here, I think it'll be so much harder to stop him from being re-elected. You know how Cheney and Rumsfeld have their whole 'our country good, other countries bad' thing going—if Bush wins, he'll probably pick on some random country and go to war—and you know how the Americans—and sure, they may be alone in the world in this, but it's their way—how they refuse to can an incompetent president if he's gotten them into a war that can't be won and which slowly kills their citizens.

I know, John. Fear of being labeled unpatriotic or something.

Yeah. So I just thought this would be so much easier. I guess I wasn't thinking of how my actions might affect another agent. I'm sorry.

Aw, hey—it's okay. I'm sure I would have done the same thing in your shoes. There's got to be….hmmm. I mean…is there maybe a third candidate we could both work to get elected? So we can maybe use each other's strengths—you know, work together to achieve both our goals?

That's a great idea, John. But, no—I'm afraid this is a two party system. Just the two candidates.

Really? That doesn't make sense. What year did they vote

out the multi-party system?

They didn't. Actually, they never—

Oh, hey look, there's John. Hey, John! Over here.

Hi, John. Hello, John. How are you guys?

Great.

We're here on assignment—how about you, John.

Oh, me? Yeah, assignment. I don't mind telling—I know I can trust you guys. I've been selected to eliminate democracy. I figured the 2000 election would be a good place to start. Oh, wait—there goes Nader. I've got to keep him out of the debates—well, okay. *I* don't need to—the Democrats and Republicans are doing that for me. I tell you—this assignment is *so* easy. I mean, just wait until you hear what they've cooked up with this Patriot Act. Hey, great to see you, guys, but I better go catch up.

That guy gets all the good assignments.

No kidding. So anyway—what were you saying, John?

Yes, you were talking about the multi-party system.

Oh, yeah. They don't have it. Two parties control everything.

You're kidding, right? I mean—surely it's not possible that everyone in the entire country falls into one of these two camps.

Well, close enough. They don't complain about it.

Well, shit. That means both candidates are dang near encouraged to move to the center—to get the votes of anyone in the middle. That would box out any third party candidates —making them look like the bad guy.

Tell me about it.

135

Damn. Big modern country like this, you'd think they'd have their shit together.

.   .   .

In the future, humans will be unable to travel to the past to save the present.

One of the obvious requirements for time travel is yogurt, lots of it. The science is fairly complicated, so most people get confused by its purpose. Contrary to popular understanding, the yogurt is not a fuel for the time machine. Rather, the yogurt functions more as a lubricant for the gears that korelemn the stipnods. Only yogurt—with its unique consistency, texture, and viscosity can provide the appropriate tension.

And what if you run without it? Well, try running a car with no oil for several months. And now realize that anytime people want to time travel, they are probably going out for at least a few years—sometimes centuries or millennia. Yes, scooting from 2540 down to the Renaissance is exactly like driving a car with no oil for 1000 years. Can't be done.

Other substances have been tried out, but nothing worked. Okay, that's not completely true. Early on, one man designed a time machine engine that ran on one of the byproducts of the yogurt production process. But pretty soon the yogurt companies bought out his design, flooded the market with their product, and killed him.

Even though the U.S. represented 4% of the population of the earth at the time, they took over 80% of the yogurt, with the majority of that used by the U.S. government's Department of Private Land Acquisition.

Realizing they had erred in slowly selling off bits and pieces of National Forests, National Parks, and National Monuments—until all they were left with was Yosemite which no one wanted due to all the pollution—the U.S. embarked on an ambitious initiative to reclaim land from public ventures—highways, schools, parks, sewage treatment plants, liquor stores, casinos, putt-putt courses, office parks, etc.

They initially tried the old-fashioned way: eminent domain. But the attempts ended up in courts—courts that were increasingly supportive of private citizen's rights to own the property that they already owned. So the government decided to just get the land first. Any land they had an eye on, they studied their records to see when the land last switched hands cheaply. Then they zoomed on back, plopped down some moolah, and sat on the land. Then they popped back to the present and wala! They've got the rights.

But all that travel takes a lot of yogurt. Activists bemoan the ransacking of mother earth—yogurt is her lifeblood and it is being stolen, rendered nonexistent. Scientists make dire predictions about the end of yogurt. The U.S. is using up the supply much faster than it can be replenished. And when it is gone, there will be none left. Politicians line up on either side of the debate, though both sides lecture their colleagues about how the yogurt must be protected.

No one believes. Or no one wants to believe. The scientists are routinely ignored, discredited, sacked from government payrolls, lampooned in the papers and on late-night talk shows, and their cars are keyed.

Peak yogurt is reached in 2799. From there, it is downhill fast.

With the supply dwindling, and prices skyrocketing, attempts are made to travel back to the days of yogurt and carry it forward. The assumption being that if you brought back a tanker of yogurt and only needed a few gallons to travel, the rest should arrive with you neatly. But this fails.

This ignores the fact that yogurt is a dairy product, and as such, if left out for a few days, it starts to go bad. And bad yogurt will get a time machine nowhere fast. Sure, you can take several quarts with you and they'll keep for your trip. But if you take more than you need, it'll be bad by the time your Filby is back safe in the present.

The attempts to bring forward more yogurt just use up even more. The end comes faster.

On top of this, people began stockpiling their yogurt, hoarding their supply, demanding outrageous sums even for the lowest grade non-organic fruit-on-the-bottom varieties. Despite the crunch felt by the average citizen, the yogurt companies themselves show record profits. The government discusses ways to bring relief to the people, but no proposal is acceptable to all. They do nothing.

Then early in May 2832, the day arrives. On a Saturday afternoon, the earth's yogurt supply is gone. Poof. Just like that.

Filby XJs just a few years old are traded away for used paperbacks, day-old bagels, or pocket change; older models are left on the street, worth far less than the materials used to build them.

.　.　.

God, I finally made it. Next time, I'm getting a fucking car. I'm getting too old for this public transportation shit. I probably shouldn't have gone back so far in time to start with —the 60's, what the high holy hell was I thinking? Now that I have all the experience and know-how to be the ideal president, I don't know if I have the energy.

Well, if anything, the experience should make me a stronger candidate. And with the resume I've got—water pollution, nursing homes, airline deregulation, heck—I'm a walking consumer advocating machine! Take that. I should get a tattoo that reads "Advocate this, motherfucker!" Anyway, with my record, no wankjob could possibly vote against me. Now, to the debate. Mental note: watch the language, Ralph.

Excuse me, kind sir. I'm here for the presidential debate.

Can I see your ticket?

Ticket? Oh—golly! That's a joke! Very good, very good, sir. So where is my dressing room? Is it backstage?

What?

The dressing room? You know—as they say in the biz, please point me to the green room. Listen, do they have Evian back there?

I'm sorry, sir. But without a ticket, I can't let you in.

Oh—you weren't joking. Gosh, I guess I didn't make

myself clear. My sincere apologies. Let me begin again. Excuse me, kind sir. I'm here for the presidential debate—but not to *watch* the debates. I'm here to *participate*. You see, I'm Ralph Nader.

I don't care who you are, sir. I can not let you in without a ticket.

Ralph, Ralph! Here—take mine! Here's a ticket.

What, oh—thank you, young man. Very generous. Alright. Here you are then. Ahem. Now let me in and point me to my dressing room!

Uh huh…uh huh…will do, over and out. That was my superior. He says I can not let you in here, ticket or no ticket.

Most preposterous, I say! I am a presidential candidate and this is the presidential debate.

You were not invited, sir. The rules are clear: My superior says you need to poll at least five percent to be invited.

Wonderful! I daresay I'm running at seven percent according to some polls.

Oh—did I say five percent? I meant fifteen percent. You have to be at fifteen percent. And what were you running at again? I thought so. Now move along, sir.

Hey, now. You're being a bit pushy, kind sir.

Guards—over here. This man refuses to leave.

You can't stop me. I'm Ralph fucking Nader!

Yeah, yeah. Tell it to the debate committee.

And I have a ticket. Bitch!

.   .   .

In the past, the present preceded the future.

There is a psychological component to time, one in which people believe the past is predicated to have already happened and the future to have not happened yet. This is in part because people have a strong belief that the universe follows well-defined rules, and all of human history to this point has not defined a rule that allows the future to precede the past or for the present to coexist with the past or future.

But now scientists aren't so sure. One of the few things that can change well-defined rules is time. The universe revolves around the earth. Lead can be turned into gold. Nothing can escape from a black hole. All once well-defined rules. Now not so defined.

Nothing changes the rules like knowledge. And as we come to a greater understanding of time, the rules will be rewritten.

Current theories advance the possibility that the past and future have never existed, only the present (presentism); that the past and present exist but that the future does not exist (the growing block theory); that the past and the future exist eternally (eternalism); and that the past, present, and future all exist simultaneously in one single space-time (four dimensionalism).

However, none of these is quite accurate. It will take several hundred years for humans to develop a full understanding of time, but by 2412, it will be understood that time is actually a loop. Yes, the past precedes the present which precedes the future, but the future precedes the past.

There is no other possibility.

.　　.　　.

"Big day Tuesday. Feeling any jitters?"

"What, me? No. I think we'll do just fine. And then my Dad will never lecture me again."

"What's that, Dick? Your Dad?"

"What? Oh nothing, George. Just thinking of my old man. I think he'd really be proud of me tonight. I'll tell you—I used to be a tremendous jerk-off. Mostly sitting around drinking beer with my best friend. Kimo. My only friend, really."

"Well, nothing wrong with that." George smiled. "I've certainly done my share of jerking off."

"Um…too much information, George."

"Oh, sorry. I meant, metaphorlicky. I guess sometimes I don't know what to say without my speechwriter. Ha ha."

"Well, when time brings us back to this conversation again, please just say you've done your share of drinking. It'll go over much better."

"Thanks for the tip, Dick. You know, you've been so great —ever since you started babysitting for me. It's been a lot of fun. And I want you to know that even if we lose this election, it's been great, and you and Rummy can still come over and we can play Space Invaders."

"Thanks, George. But as I was saying. Since I arrived in DC, I've been a changed man. I've been working toward something important, really accomplishing something big. I had a goal, I put my mind to it, I worked my tail off, George, and mostly I didn't even have to resort to a few well-placed phone calls to accomplish my goals. And here we are today, on the brink of victory."

"To the victors, go the spoils. But I hope they're not all spoiled! Ha ha! Get it?"

"George."

"Yes, Dick."

"Shut up."

"Sorry. So I guess once we're in, you guys are going to want to start planning the whole Iraq invasion now."

"What plans? Who needs plans? We'll figure out a reason for invading. Then we'll invade. That's that. That's planning for you. But we'll leave that to Rummy—you still okay with him as your SecDef?"

"Oh, sure. I've said it before and I'll say it again: Whatever you say, Dick. You know more about these things than I ever will."

"Thank you, George. That's greatly appreciated."

"It's the least I could do for the best babysitter ever."

"Remember what I said. You can't ever tell anyone that in public."

"I know, I know. I'll keep it to myself."

"Thank you."

"But the girls do really love you. Say, Laura and I were hoping to get away next Saturday—do you think you could come over then?"

"Man, this is going to be great, George. Just a few more days until it's all done. I tell you, ever since my friend Kimo invited me along on that vacation—"

"Kimo, eh? Would that be Kimo Levernson?"

"What? Do you know him?"

"Oh, sure."

"Wait—smallish guy, glasses. Kinda greasy hair. Maybe a few pimples. That him?"

"Yeah, though I'm not sure about the pimples. He's working on the Gore campaign, but I know him from Sheila Watterly. He's dating her daughter, Faith."

"Shit. He's working *for* the Gore campaign? Shit, shit."

"What's wrong? What did I say?"

"Get Rove on the line. Now."

. . .

So, is this a surprise? That I see you, and yet the work is not done.

I'm sorry. I can't do it.

My, my. Something must be quite wrong for you to suffer a delusion that you can just walk away from a deal.

I have a fear. It may be that all the pain and suffering in the world originates in Gore's presidency.

And I assure you, dearie, it most certainly does.

But I fear we may be making a bigger mistake. What if whoever is elected in place of him actually causes *more* pain and suffering? How would we know?

Ha! Surely, you jest! More pain and suffering than *all* the pain and suffering? I'm not even sure that is possible.

I guess it's not even that—I'm not necessarily worried about the pain. Fine if we eliminate the pain and suffering. But what if something else changes.

What if *what*? Whatever are you talking about?

I just feel it may be wrong to change history. There may be unforeseen circumstances.

Unforeseen circumstances? Why—if you want to see the circumstances, just fly into the future. See for yourself the result. And, hmmm. Circumstance doesn't seem like quite the right word. Try...oh, yes. Consequences. Yes, much better. If you want to see the consequences—go see. I'll wait here.

But that's just it—I can't see the consequences until history has been changed. You can't see the consequence of removing Gore until Gore is removed. That's the problem with history.

I'm not sure it's a problem with history so much as a personal problem. I mean—I certainly don't have a problem with it. I'm not even sure what your problem is. Tell me this again.

You don't get it. If we as a society vote to remove something every six years, we may be losing a longer term value of an item. A value that may not appear until after we've already eliminated it.

You're not making sense, dear. If we've already eliminated it, then there will be no value.

Exactly. That's exactly what I'm saying. Like, what if we vote to remove the Irish potato famine—

I assure you, it will never happen. I know their ad man personally and he—

Okay, bad example. But, how about this. What if the world had developed this vote by 2108 and had decided we had no use for boysenberry marmalade? Not the best example, I admit. But after the yogurt ran out, if we had learned that boysenberry marmalade was an appropriate substitute, but we had *already* eliminated it, then we would have eliminated something that had a value later on. And perhaps we are doing that now. What if the Gore presidency has a value to the year 3416 that we don't know about? What if Yoko meeting John has a value to 4488 and we have not advanced as a society to be able to know exactly what that is?

Good lord, think about what you're saying. What if there is an unforeseen value to slavery? To nuclear warheads and terrorism and the Nazi holocaust! Unseen value? No, no, no. No, it is truly a wonder that we have eliminated these terrible things—you should delight that these are gone, but here you are lamenting them. Please don't tell me you would have them all back.

I don't disagree. Yes, we have done a service to human-kind by eliminating them. But I'm not convinced that everything that has been eliminated has proved so terrible. Nuclear warheads and terrorism are one thing. But toy guns?

Representative of the real thing—programming kids at an early age to embrace violence.

What about video games?

Responsible for generations of youth not being able to explore the great open spaces.

Well, how about the great open spaces? They've been eliminated, too.

A gathering place for youth, where they can congregate and plot to overturn the established order.

And peanut butter?

Try telling this to all the people with peanut allergies—

oh, why am I defending every little thing. I didn't vote for half of these. But that doesn't mean they are good and should have been saved.

No. But it doesn't make them evil either.

Listen, Apple. Are you going to do it or not. Just tell me. If you can't, fine. Go home. I'll find someone who I can trust to carry out the assignment.

Thank you. But I can't do it.

Alright. Get out of here, I have work to do.

By the way, Hill. I was rather surprised to see you in the car that day. That wasn't random, was it?

Like I said—I'll find someone who can carry out the assignment. Now if you don't mind, I have to go get a job at a high school in Natrona 2780.

.   .   .

"I've got a problem, Karl. I'm going to need some of your best stuff. One-hundred percent pure if you got it. I need it bad, man. Can you set me up?"

"Whoa, slow down there. Let's start over. Now tell me, Dick. What's your poison?"

"Spin, of course. I really need it. You can help me, can't you?"

"No worries, Dick. I am your spinning mack daddy. I am your spin ninja—your spinja. You could call me the spin master. If I was a salad, I'd be a salad spinner. If I was infinity, I'd be spinning infinity. If I was a 70's Motown group singing about rubber bands and/or Sadie, I'd be—"

"Karl. I really hate when you do that. Please stop."

"Sorry, Dick. Tell me what's on your mind."

"Well, I just learned that ██████████████████ ██. I think ████████████████████████████████████. Worse, ████████████████████████████████████ ████████████████████████████. The problem is █ ██. ████████████████████████████ Maybe I can ████ ██ ██."

"My advice? Don't mention any of it. Just black it out, Dick."

"You think?"

"Yes. By the way, great title. Not sure what the Captain part signifies, though. Maybe consider changing the name. Something generic like 'In My Time' would work well. Just be sure to have an equally generic subtitle, maybe 'A Personal and Political Memoir.'"

"Explain something to me, Karl. If I leave all that out, then how would my tell-all memoir be tell-all?"

"I don't know, Dick. But if you want me to help you, you have to work with me. Now can you promise me it stays out of the memoir?"

"Yes, fine. Anything. I'll block it out. Now would you get me some spin, please? I'm dying here."

"Alright, I'm on it. Give me an hour. I'll take care of everything."

.   .   .

In the present, you are having trouble believing any of this could possibly be true.

If this is the case, very likely you are reading this story sometime prior to 2016. As far as you know, time travel is a thing of the future—it hasn't been invented yet.

And that may be true. It may be that time travel has not been invented yet. And yes, this may pose a problem for the author of this work completing all his research, as he has found that many of his sources have not been created yet. This has slowed him down immensely, meaning that he may not meet his deadline. Do not hold this against him. Rather, you might just consider applauding his efforts. When some of the author's sources, such as *A People's History of Liebermanbot* and *Richard Scarry's Big Book of Richard Perle*, will not be created for eight hundred years, it is the dedicated writer who continues forging ahead, in the hopes of creating a coherent narrative for the reader. He should be commended for pushing on in the face of such a daunting, seemingly impossible task.

But fear not, dear reader. For even if it takes eight *thousand* years, this writer will complete the research and get the book out. You deserve nothing less. Yes, it is that important.

However, do bear in mind that the lack of the availability of time travel today will not stop people from 2252, 3146, or 4307 from traveling backward in time. And so this fact does not clear you from any responsibility for saving someone from the future. In fact, at the U.N. Convention in Budapest 2341, just this issue will be debated. It will be decided that all individuals of all nations have a responsibility to their fellow human beings, to respond when approached for help, regardless of age, gender, race, nationality, ability, sexual preference, or era. Even if you believe it is perfectly acceptable and legal in your own country and your own time, you can be tried in absentia if proceedings are brought against you in any nation that which will be a signatory to the Budapest Conventions.

Just as you can't commit war crimes in Germany or Yugoslavia and expect that you won't be tried in the Hague, you can't ignore someone's plea for help in 2011 or 2016 and expect that you won't be tried in 2145 or 3406.

So if someone shows up at your house and asks you to help them save the future, realize it *is* your responsibility. You have no choice. If, in approximately thirty-four minutes, you hear a knock at the door, run to the door. Do not dawdle. It could be a matter of life or death.

If that person has a goatee and his hair in a pony-tail and he is wearing a flannel shirt, know that he bears the uniform of the future. Help him help you.

In fact, it may be that the man has run low on yogurt or perhaps marmalade or BBQ sauce. Perhaps he wants to help you, this man from the future, but he just needs a little fuel.

Give him the yogurt.

.   .   .

I should note that it might be quite a bit more than thirty-four minutes, depending on what time he left the future, his present rate of speed, and whether he stops along the way to fill up or waits until after his visit to your door in order to fill up. Or perhaps he may have a breakdown on the Interyear and not get there for a few months.

Still, be kind to him.

.   .   .

From the Journal of Dick Cheney

November 4, 2000

Damn. I can't believe Kimo beat me to it. Working from within the campaign to defeat Gore. How could I be so stupid to think I would be the only one to realize I had the opportunity to fulfill my old man's wishes? Obviously he wants all the glory for himself. Wants to keep me from being a hero to all the people of the future.

Yes—as often as he was over my house, he heard Dad's lectures almost as much as I did. In fact, I think Dad often waited until there was an audience of two before we got into it. And that second would have been Kimo. And surely Kimo saw my Dad as a second father. I bet he would do anything to please my old man—never mind how I may feel about it.

But why desert me? Why not work with me? We could have done this together. And what do I do now? I've been working 31 years for this moment, and now he may take all the credit.

Can I live with this? Is this okay? I mean, what if I stop him and somehow end up stopping whatever he has instituted to keep Gore from winning? What if I inadvertently throw the election *to* Gore, by stopping Kimo? Wouldn't it be better to just let Kimo do what he's going to do? Maybe even celebrate his victory with him over a few Buds.

I have to think about this.

November 5, 2000

A horrible thought occurred to me last night. What if Kimo is really working *for* Gore. Oh, diary, tell me it can't be true. This is Kimo. Could he be against everything I have worked so hard for?

Well, if he is working for Gore, then I have no choice but to stop him. Decisions, decisions.

Dammit, this is foolproof! I will win this election, Kimo or no Kimo.

Please forgive me, Kimo, for what I am about to do. You may be my best friend 700 years from now, but it's time for one of those well-placed phone calls.

November 6, 2000

Shit, why haven't they called? It should have been done hours ago. Could something have gone wrong? No. These guys are the best there are. And we're just dealing with Kimo here. Unless...oh, I hope he hasn't offered them more money to come back and kill me off. If he's with Gore's people, he probably has the resources. Shit. That would totally ruin this day.

Oh, but what if he anticipated it. He obviously knows I'm working against Gore. I mean, I'm only at the head of the Republican Party ticket. I know he's heard. He must have heard, right?

Here it is, election day. The day I've been working toward for half my life. Soon I will be President, er, I mean Vice President, of course. Just a little slip there. Heh heh heh. But soon I will be V.P. and the world will be free from the treachery that was the Al Gore presidency.

But why haven't they called? What is keeping them?

Damn, damn, damn.

What is going on?

. . .

In the future, all citizens of the world will see the same commercials.

They will gather around their kaxcurtipods to watch the premiere of the latest straight-to-kaxcurtipod Hollywood blockbuster. And they will all watch each of the fourteen or so commercial advertisements prior to the film.

All the people of the world will learn that only Cancer Sticks Lite with LoTar can "keep you semi-de-stressed while also giving you less than a thirty-three percent chance of dying from lung cancer." They will all learn that the new Toybox18 video game system will be released soon. They will all learn that the new VideoGamer23 video game system will be released very very soon. And they will all learn that the new GamerGame video game system will be released very very very soon.

They will all see a preview for the upcoming reality series *The Real World War IX: Orange County*, which offers seven beautiful twenty-somethings the opportunity to live in a colorful beach house together and determine which country to attack to begin the next World War. They will all view the latest ad from the Committee in Favor of Eliminating the Irish Potato Famine, after which they will all wonder why exactly "it's right for the potato." And they will all wonder, What does that even mean? They will all find that sexy Thai action star Jennifer Palevengklin prefers Dentubright with new Floristat8. And they will all learn that Coca-Cola would like to teach the world to sing.

But just as they are ready for the movie, just as they have lost count of how many ads they have viewed—for everyone keeps count: "Was that 12 or 13?"—they will see the splashy ad and hear the catchy jingle written and performed by Softer Hobby during their recent reunion tour.

> Feeling pain? You want more?
> You can have it with Al Gore.
> Can't get up from down on the floor?
> You'll stay there, if you
> Stay with Gore (x2)
> And if you are feeling poor,
> Landlord kickin' you out the door,
> Nothing to do, and now you're bored,
> Cuz you can't afford to go to the store or a whore
> Blame Gore! (x4)

Tired of war? Want no more.

Too bad, you'll get it if you

Pick Gore. Pick Gore.

(spoken:) This election day, consider this: During his presidency, Al Gore took steps to ensure all the pain and suffering of everyone in the world. So if you are feeling the least hint of discomfort, you owe it to yourself to vote out the presidency of Gore, 43rd U.S. president. Because without Gore, we'd always have Paris.

(with music:) No more Gore! For shore! (x2)

(spoken again:) Paid for by the Committee to Eliminate the Gore Presidency from History.

When all those consumers turn off their kpods and go to the polls, they won't remember much. But they will see Gore's name and think this: *Can't get up from down on the floor? You'll stay there, if you stay with Gore.*

And they will vote in record numbers.

· · ·

"Kimo!"

"Hello, Dick. Long time, no see."

"Yes. Long time."

"I tried calling you."

"Don't give me excuses. You never called."

"But I did. I could never get through, though. I left message after message with the White House switchboard. I take it you didn't get them."

"You really tried to reach me?"

"Of course, you're my best friend. Or...you were."

"Kimo, don't give me a guilt trip. I woke up that day and you were gone. I had to get on with my life. Where have you been all these years?"

"Where have I been? Oh, here and there. Mostly alternating between DC through the 70's, 80's, and 90's. And Nantes 1847."

"But how?"

"Same way we got here—I had a time machine, remember?"

"But the Filby was out of yogurt. I saw it with my own eyes."

"Correction. It was half-out of yogurt. You saw it with your own eyes."

"But you told me—You lied to me?"

"No, no. At the time it was standard. Half empty equals empty. But when I woke up from my drunken stupor—I woke up before you—I remembered a dream I had. I mean, when we left, every company had their own standards: with Filby, half empty was empty. With Yleuro, two-thirds empty was empty. With the Druylk, half empty was half full. And so on. In my dream, somehow our story becomes known to future generations—that you and I were stuck here due to the confusion with the gas tank. And then someone did something about it. Apparently this guy saw to it that there would be an industry standard of half-empty equaling half-empty, fully empty equaling fully empty."

"Hey—good idea."

"Yeah. But when I woke up that day, I slowly came to realize that it wasn't a dream. It was a memory. Because whoever this guy is made the industry standard based on us getting stuck in 1969, then the change was implemented way before we left in 2791. I mean, it could have been implemented hundreds of years before we left. Meaning that as I stood there in 1969, our Filby was sitting out on that road with a half-tank of yogurt.

"Still thinking it might possibly be a dream, I ran out there to check the car. Sure enough, it was good to go. I drove straight back to our hotel as fast I could, so I could wake you up and we could continue on to Nantes. But, you weren't there, Dick. You were in the Nixon administration."

"I still don't know how that happened," Dick laughed.

"You know, it's ironic. Once you became a public servant. it made it near impossible to get through to you."

"Well, I'm glad you finally made it to Nantes. How was it?"

"Not so hot. I mean, sure there are some really fine ladies —just as we'd heard. But I could never develop a lasting relationship with anyone there. I had no friends."

"Really? That's not like you—everyone likes you."

"I know. But I needed to be in DC in case you called. So I'd hit Nantes for a day or two—sometimes three—rarely three. But then I'd pop back to DC. Check my messages. Wait by the phone."

"You mean all these years, I could have found you. And we could have returned to 2791? Together? We could have been back sipping our Buds—all these years."[*]

"All you had to do was click your heels together. And then get off your ass and go check your messages. Well, and then give me a call, and take a ride with me on the Filby express. By the way, Katie Driscoll asked about you."

"You went back? To Natrona?"

"Yeah, a couple times. It's not the same without you, though. Hillyer keeps getting weirder. My grades keep slipping. It seems like history keeps changing between when we take a test and when the test is graded."

"How's my dad?"

"Oh, he's the same. The one constant. He still says we need to bring down Gore."

"Did he ask about me?"

"Not exactly. Mostly we talk strategy. I ask him what he would do if he could zip down to 2000 and secretly infiltrate the Gore campaign. He has some great ideas. If you talked to him about it for a few minutes, you'd be surprised what his thoughts are on the whole thing. Just last week, we were sipping some beer."

"Wait a minute—you sat around drinking Buds with my dad?"

"Not exactly. We drink this new kind. It's called Bud^{Bud}. Or Bud squared. Well, some people call it Bud squared. But most people in the know use the 'Bud-to-the-Bud.' Yeah. Since you've forgotten about me, he's probably my best

---

[*] Cue "Paris Walked Away" by Alan Rose, from the Love Earth Music soundtrack *music from and inspired by the novel* Dick Cheney Saves Paris.

friend. Your dad is the closest thing I have to you."

"My dad? Kimo. I'm sorry. This has been. I. I don't know what to say. Other than...I missed you."

"By the way, you can have this back." Kimo handed him a gun.

"What's this?" And then Dick realized. His well-placed phone call.

"Don't give me your miss-me bullcrap, Dick. You tried to...you tried to kill me. My best friend."

"I'm sorry, Kee. I thought you were working against me." Dick looked at the gun and then set it on the table. "Are you?"

"Dick. You know I'm working from within—don't you? I mean, I only went into politics to get closer to you. Surely, you don't think I secretly want Gore to win."

"Wouldn't be so secret—you're on his campaign."

"Dude—how could I ever want him to win? Thanks to your dad, it is so ingrained in my subconscious that all the pain and suffering in the entire world is a result of Al Gore winning this election. I mean, shit. If getting stood up at homecoming by Roxie Turtlmichal, or if getting a C in History, or if...if learning that my best friend is trying to kill me, if all this suffering can be stopped by electing anyone but Gore, then I'm all for it."

"Tell me, Kimo. How exactly do you keep that secret in an organization dedicated to electing Gore? If you're against him like you say you are, then the first time you do something against the campaign, you'd be booted from the team. So that leaves me to believe you haven't done shit for defeating him."

"You're wrong. It may be that I've had to be careful and keep my politics to myself. But actually quite a number of guys on the team want to see Gore lose. I haven't told them my thoughts—I've been playing it smart. I have accomplished a few things already—I've just been good at letting my colleagues deal with the fallout. They hate Gore so much, they've been stumbling over themselves to take credit for my successes. Sure, they get canned. But they're excited to go blog about how they caused some problem or other. Like how they were on the Gore/Lieberman campaign and answered the phone 'Bore/Need-a-man campaign.' Or about how they took all the pencils from the room."

"All the pencils, huh?" Dick smiled. "That's pretty good. It does sound like you're doing some good work. I'm sorry I doubted you."

"Well, I don't know if I can trust you, just yet. And it probably won't help me to be seen talking to you this close to the election. But, Dick. I do know this probably means more to you than me. I mean—you lived with your ol' man forever. For me, he's a drinking buddy. Someone to talk to, watch some Natrona football with."

"Ah, the Mighty Fighting 'Bolders."

"So if there's anything I can do for you—don't hesitate."

"Thank you, Kimo. That means a lot."

They hugged.

·   ·   ·

On CBS, Dan Rather says, "We would rather be last than be wrong. If we say somebody's carried a state, you can pretty much take it to the bank."

The Associated Press calls Kentucky and Indiana in Bush's favor.

Voter News Service, a group pooling resources of ABC, CBS, CNN, Fox, NBC, and the AP, calls Florida for Gore.

On ABC, Peter Jennings says, "Al Gore wins the state of Florida and its 25 electoral votes. It gives him the first big state momentum of the evening."

Dan Rather says Bush's prospects are "shakier than cafeteria Jell-o."

Voter News Service retracts its call for the state of Florida going to Gore.

CNN moves Florida to Undecided. Other networks quickly follow.

Dan Rather says, "To err is human, but to really foul up requires a computer."

On Fox News, George Bush's first cousin John Ellis projects Florida, and therefore the presidency, for Bush.

On CNN, Bernard Shaw says, "George Bush, Governor of Texas, will become the 43rd President of the United States. At eighteen minutes past two o'clock eastern time, CNN declares that George Walker Bush has won Florida's 25 electoral votes and this should put him over the top."

Al Gore calls Bush to concede, congratulating him on his win. Gore leaves his Nashville hotel to address a crowd of supporters. He never makes it. Before he arrives, the 50,000 vote margin for Bush narrows to few thousand.

On NBC, Tom Brokaw says, "That would be something if the networks managed to blow it twice in one night."

Al Gore calls Bush to un-concede. Reports label it a heated exchange, with Gore retracting his concession. CNN reports the margin is now 1300 votes.

NBC and CBS retract their earlier call for Bush.

Gore captures the popular vote. If he keeps it and loses Florida, he will be the fourth to win the popular vote but lose the presidency, after Andrew Jackson, who lost to John Quincy Adams in 1824; Samuel Tildin, who lost to Rutherford B. Hayes in 1876; and Grover Cleveland, who lost to Benjamin Harrison in 1888.

.   .   .

In the past, it was thought that yogurt was necessary for time travel. But in the future the truth will come out.

It won't happen until 3416, but by that time much blood will be spilled. Several democratically elected heads of states will be deposed and several world wars will be fought over it. The worst will be the Yogurt Putsch of 2801. The Eurasian Union will unite against the United States (and Canada) of America of in the worst battle the earth has seen since the Dannon-Yoplait War of 2750.

In Chouli 3228, a team of Amish scientists will learn to harness the power of boysenberry marmalade. However, due to the insular nature of their communities, it will take more than a century for it to leak out—the Amish have discovered the latest fuel and their children are joyriding their horse-drawn carts through history.

There will be scandal, with editorials questioning their patriotism: Why didn't they tell us sooner? Why do the Amish hate us so? Is it our freedom they hate? The U.S. government will round up these terrorists and ferry them to an undisclosed prison where they can be tortured in order to learn what other secrets they may harbor—secrets which may pose a national security threat.

In reality, the Amish will think themselves the last to know. They will have no idea that there is any secret about the marmalade, until the day that stream of paddy wagons comes tearing into town. For scientific journals will have theorized about marmalade for hundreds of years before Amish farmer Nils Jorberdssonsson happens across one such journal while enjoying a fried bologna sandwich at Henrik Johnson's Country Market in Berlin, Ohio, soon after having his beard trimmed. Later that day, Nils's son Nilsson will come home with an old Filby XJ dragged behind his carriage.

"What do you got there, my good son?"

"I found it out on Pater Miller's farm. I do believe it a time machine!"

"Oh, hey then," Nils will say. "I may have the proper thing to get it running. If you can bring me some of mama's best boysenberry marmalade."

And so will begin years of good fun for the Amish teens of Holmes County, Ohio. Hopping over to the famous Andersson barn raising in 2312 or the great cheese wheel of 2106 or even sneaking into the Sadie Hawkins Dance over in the big city in 1973.

Nils will never travel far outside of Holmes County, so as far as he will be concerned, if he can read it in a journal, it must be fairly common knowledge. But in reality, the scientific journals will not be widely read. Sure, studies will show that fuels other than yogurt should work fine—perhaps even better than yogurt. But the yogurt companies themselves will suppress this information. They will offer their own studies that prove beyond a shadow of doubt, that only yogurt will work in a time machine. And they will buy up every copy of any journal that dares disagree. Well, except for one copy, accidentally sent to Pers Andersson. Pers was the owner of the Andersson Country Market in Berlin, Ohio, which later passed upon Pers' death to Henrik Johnson, including all fixtures, machinery, signs, and all inventory. And one copy of *Science Week*.

Once it is clear to citizens of the future that boysenberry marmalade works just as well as blackberry yogurt, and that it is not a conspiracy on the part of Amish teenagers, there will be movements to pardon all Amish of any wrongdoing. Movements for public apologies. For a national day of reconciliation, whereby all Amish will be invited to the nation's capital to attend a gala ball thrown by the president in their honor.

But the Amish will not attend the parties or the national day of reconciliation. They will just want to get back to plowing the fields and raising more barns. Of course, for ignoring the celebration, their patriotism will be called into question. But let all who question their heart, know the real truth: the Amish love their country as much as any entire group of people can be said to love their country.

Still later, it will come out that not only boysenberry marmalade but other food items can power time machines. Equally as effective are honey BBQ sauce packets from fast food chain BurgerTopia, and pretty much any fast food condiment and/or breakfast item with a sugar content that exceeds 14 kurtliwds.

.   .   .

"Oh, they're hugging. How charming."

"Mr. Hillyer!"

Kimo glanced at Dick, wondering why he was being so formal. Dick understood Kimo's glance. "It's a long story," he said.

"So here you are together again—for the first time. Sorry to interrupt your little reunion. And are we plotting our whole 'Gore loses' campaign? Spare me, boys. There is nothing you can do now to keep Gore from winning."

"You—you've been working against us since before we even left Natrona."

"No, only since we arrived. I had a little chat with a common friend of ours and it gave me something to think about. During our ride to 1969, I paid very careful attention to the history we were passing. And now I need to stop you."

"Why, Hillyer? Why do you want Gore to win?"

"If you paid any attention at all during the ride, you would have seen. Gore fixed things. He made things right. In his first term, he took away our pain and suffering—from everyone around the world. He made it so people had nothing to worry about. Everyone had a home. Everyone had a home cooked meal. Everyone had a living wage and everyone had free internet at filling stations. Al Gore did this!"

"No!" said Dick. "You're lying. If he took away all this pain and suffering, as you say, how could so many people fault him for *bringing* all the pain and suffering in the world."

"God—that ridiculous Paris incident. Which was quite exciting to see, I should add. I wish they had instant replay in those machine. Though I suppose if we would have just backed up—"

"You were saying?"

"Oh, sorry. The people hated Gore for one terrible incident on one day. With everything they ever needed, people stopped suffering. They stopped feeling pain. But they still had a terrible urge to feel pain. They missed it. After century upon century of human suffering, the people *needed* to suffer. So they tried to recall a painful moment from our history. The media locked on to that Paris incident."

"It kinda makes sense, Dick."

"Shut up, Kimo. It can't be true."

"Oh, but it is true," said Hillyer. "Paris Hilton, vaporized. And the people had a reason to feel again. To feel the pain of losing Paris. So *of course* all the pain and suffering is rooted in Gore's first term—if knowing that Paris Hilton has been vaporized is all that you have to feel pain about, that is."

"See—it *is* Gore's fault. And that's why he has to go."

"Ah, but Gore was against it from the start. He didn't have the political will to shut down the program once it began.

However, you have now started us down the road toward unlimited presidential powers, Dick. Mr. Gore thanks you, by the way. They will serve him well."

Kimo looked at Dick. "You—you're responsible for the expansion of presidential authority?"

"Tell him, Dick. Tell him what you did as head of the House Intelligence Committee. Tell him how you worked with your Republican colleagues to sacrifice truth and honesty when our country needed it most—just to protect your high-level cronies. And now Al Gore will use his expanded authority not only to halt the flawed time travel program, but to roll back road building and logging in national forests, to end oil-drilling in Alaska, to expand health coverage for all children and seniors, to regulate industrial pollution and to raise educational standards for all —all things he was unable to accomplish the last time he was elected in 2000. Bwah-ha-ha! All because you, Dick Cheney, have worked to expand presidential authority!"

"Is this all true, Dick?"

"Yes, Dick. Is it true? Tell Kimo that you did it all—all of this!—in exchange for a measly B in History."

"Okay, well that I can understand. That makes sense."

"Really? So no hard feelings, Kimo?"

"No hard feelings, Dick."

"And it's too late to do anything about it, boys. The election is tomorrow."

Dick had a fleeting thought. The Supreme Court. It wasn't too late.

"Oh, and Dick. In Nantes? The ladies are double-fine.

Much better than your—what's her name—Lynne. Your Katie Driscoll wannabe."

"How dare you."

"See you around. Dick."

As Hillyer strolled through the door, Dick turned to grab Kimo's gun from the table, but where the gun previously sat, was a great big mound...of nothing.

"Looking for this, gentlemen?"

Dick looked up. Ralph Nader was pointing the gun at him.

Dick spoke into his left collar. "Wake up, Liebermanbot! Execute seven-dash-K. Now!"

"What the hell was that?" asked Nader. "You think mysterious proclamations into your shirt can save you, you have another think coming, you asswipes."

Just then, Joseph Lieberman walked in the door. "Hello, gentlemen. I am not a Republican."

Cheney said, "Liebermanbot, apprehend Nader."

As Nader turned toward the door, Joseph Lieberman lunged, grabbing him by the neck and smashing his head on the floor.

"Dick—stop it!"

"No. I've been working for too long at this. I need to do this. Nader is just another person who wants to see to it that I do not succeed. Again, Liebermanbot." Joseph Lieberman pounded Nader's head against the floor. "This one's for my Dad. One, more, Liebermanbot" Bam! "And this one's for Kimo. Again, Liebermanbot" BAM!

"You're killing him, Dick!"

"That may be, Kimo. But this won't stop him from being born."

Joseph Lieberman continued pounding Nader's head into the ground until it was a bloody pulp.

Just then, the door opened and Apple pie appeared.

"Just so you know, Dick. Nader was on your side."

"What? Why didn't he say so?"

"Well, you didn't exactly give him a chance before Joseph Lieberman began pounding his head into the ground. The reality is he doesn't want Gore to win any more than you. He wants to win himself—bad enough to help you stop Gore."

"Really?"

"Yes."

"But he held the gun on me. He was going to kill me."

"But he wants to kill Gore, too. And remember, Dick. The enemy of your enemy is your friend."

"I guess that makes sense."

"The truth is, you need Ralph Nader. You can't defeat Gore without him. For only Nader has the power to take votes from the progressives and liberals. Sure you've sewn up the conservative vote. But where else can you find the votes to surpass fifty percent?"

"Dammit, you're right. Well, should we tell the media about his death? If people know he's dead, they might not vote for him. And we could get those votes. But—ohmigod, the votes could go to Gore instead! We've got to do something!"

"I think our best bet is to stop his death before it happened. If Kimo still has his time machine, that is."

"Of course."

"Where is it, Kimo? We have to hurry. Before tomorrow's vote!"

"Why are you helping us, Apple pie?"

"I don't know. I'm no longer sure it's the right thing to do —changing history, that is. If it is, I have a job to do. And I don't think I can do it alone. And if it isn't, well, I trust you, Dick."

. . .

As Hillyer strolled through the door, Dick turned to grab the gun from the table, but where the gun previously sat, was a great big mound...of nothing.

Dick looked up. It was Ralph Nader.

Dick spoke into his left collar. "Wake up, Liebermanbot! Execute seven-dash-K. Now!"

"What the hell was that?" asked Nader. "You think mysterious proclamations into your shirt can save you, you have another think coming, you asswipes."

Just then, Joseph Lieberman walked in the door. "Hello, gentlemen. I am not a Republican."

Cheney said, "Liebermanbot, apprehend Nader."

As Nader turned toward the door, Joseph Lieberman lunged, grabbing him by the neck and smashing his head on the floor.

"Dick—stop it."

"No. I've been working for too long at this. I need to do this. Nader is just another person who wants to see to it that I do not succeed. Again, Liebermanbot." Joseph Lieberman pounded Nader's head against the floor. "This one's for my Dad. One, more, Liebermanbot" Bam! "And this one's for Kimo. Again, Liebermanbot" BAM!

"You're killing him, Dick!"

"That may be, Kimo. But this won't stop him from being born."

Joseph Lieberman continued pounding Nader's head into the ground until it was a bloody pulp.

Just then, the door opened and Apple pie appeared.

"No! Dick—stop it! What are you doing?"

"He was going to shoot me."

"But *I* have the gun."

"Oh. Sorry. I did think it was kind of odd when I looked over and he was just kind of standing there pointing his finger at me with a confused look on his face."

"Okay—let's try this one more time," Apple pie sighed. "To the time machine."

.   .   .

As Hillyer strolled through the door, Dick turned to grab the gun from the table, but where the gun previously sat, was a great big mound…of nothing.

Dick looked up. It was Ralph Nader.

Dick spoke into his left collar. "Wake up, Liebermanbot! Execute seven-dash-K. Now!"

"What the hell was that?" asked Nader. "You think mysterious proclamations into your shirt can save you—"

"Wait! Wait! Stop! All of you." It was Apple pie. "Before any of you shoot anyone or pound people's heads into the ground. Just stop. We need to talk."

Just then, Joseph Lieberman walked in the door. "Hello, gentlemen. I am not a Republican."

"Alright. All of you, listen up. I need you to sit down and listen to me. You guys are politicians! Sure you hate each other and all, but you should be able to find some common ground."

"If I could speak," said Dick. "I think we all have the same goal. Defeating Al Gore."

"See," said Apple pie. "That's what I'm talking about. Go on."

"I mean—I definitely want Gore to lose. I don't know about Ralph, here—"

"Fuck, yeah—that's why I'm here," said Nader.

"Hey—I want Gore to lose," said Kimo.

"And I'm pretty sure Joseph Lieberman wants Gore to lose too." To his collar, Dick whispered, "Liebermanbot, execute twenty-eight-dash-J."

"I also want Gore to lose," said Joseph Lieberman. "I am not a Republican."

"I...I don't think I can do this anymore. I'm sorry." Apple pie ran from the room.

"Apple pie—wait! Sorry, guys. I've got to catch her. I'll be right back."

In the hall, Dick caught up to her. "What's wrong—was it something I said?"

"No. It's just the whole messing with history thing. It just hit me. Hard. I think it was seeing Liebermanbot pound Nader's head into the ground—"

"And then seeing it again."

"Yeah. I know from history what a great president Lieberman becomes. And I realized he could never become that president with Nader's blood on his hands."

"But you stopped it. He doesn't have blood on his hands. You stopped me from having Joseph Lieberman kill Ralph Nader."

"But don't you see—I shouldn't have had to stop you. We shouldn't have been messing with Nader's head in the first place. This is all wrong."

"Well, I want you to know that I will never forget you. Right or wrong, I need to go. I have to stop my old teacher Hillyer from helping Gore become the next president."

"Wait—did you say Hillyer? Was he here?"

"Yeah. He left right before you showed up. I'm surprised you didn't see him on your way in."

"Wait a sec. You said he's trying to *help* Gore?"

"Yeah. He said he had a nice chat with a common friend —I'm not really sure who he was talking about, but it didn't seem like the time to ask. But I guess on the way through time he had this change of heart and now thinks Gore actually made everything great."

"You have to understand something about Hillyer. He is not who you think he is."

"I know. I thought he was simply a slightly left-leaning bike-riding hippie history teacher. But it turns out he's also a maniacal time-traveling ultra-left-wing hippie history teacher who rewards his students with high grades in order to advance a twisted social agenda."

"Okay—so you do know. He's maybe a little more than that, too. But Dick, he's very dangerous."

"I know. But I have to stop him."

"In that case, I'm going with you."

"No, I can't let you do that. You said yourself we should not mess with history. I have to do it alone."

Kimo appeared in the doorway followed by Ralph Nader and Joseph Lieberman. "No way, Dick. We can't let you fight this one alone."

Nader held out a fist. "To the cause, I offer...my experience."

Kimo covered Nader's fist with his hand and shouted, "And I give my time machine!"

Dick whispered in his collar, "Liebermanbot, execute forty-two-dash-H."

"I offer my insider connections to the Gore-Lieberman campaign," said Joseph Lieberman, adding his hand. "And I am not a Republican."

They all laughed before Dick smiled and added his own hand. "You guys are right. I could never do it on my own. Thank you."

"Hey," said Kimo. "What are friends for?"

Apple pie frowned. "I'd like to consider you a friend, too, Dick. But, you're right. I'm now convinced more than ever that we shouldn't interfere with history. I'm sorry I can't help you."

"But you have helped us, Apple pie. Remember, without

you, Ralph Nader would be dead and Al Gore might be reaping all of his votes tomorrow. You saved the world."

"I guess history will be the judge of that."

"Can I walk you out?"

"Sure, that would be fine."

"About Hillyer?" Dick asked as they strolled outside. "Should we be worried?"

"Nah. Once the election is over and Gore has lost, he'll just go back to the future and plot how he can reverse the election. But he's one of those overworked underpaid fellows. So I'm pretty sure he'll never get the time to break away again and interfere. I think your administration will be safe from the future. Well, I should probably get going. You never know how long it will take to get picked up."

"Goodbye, Apple pie. Thank you for all you've done."

"Goodbye, Dick."

Dick watched as Apple pie stuck her thumb out at the side of the road. After a minute of no cars passing by and Apple pie just standing there, thumb out, Dick felt awkward and slowly made his way back inside. There he found Kimo and Ralph deep in conversation.

"You mean there was no industry standard for what the fuel gage read—like the car could be half empty, but read full? That's totally fucked up. I mean, fine if half empty is half full. But you need a standard. Any idiot would know that."

"Exactly," said Kimo.

"Well, I think I might be able to do something about that."

"Okay, Guys. I've been working on a plan for quite some

time. It will be difficult, but with your help, I think we can do it."

They huddled together as Dick detailed the plan he'd been working out for the better part of a few decades. After much furious whispering, Kimo concluded, "I like it, Dick. It's just crazy enough to work."

"I even have a back-up plan, but that involves the Supreme Court, so it's not a sure bet."

Nader smiled. "I go hunting with those guys all the time."

"You're kidding."

"Nah. I'm a lawyer. And I've been around this town for more than forty years. Eventually you get to know everyone. In fact, a few of them owe me. Big time."

"Perfect! In that case, would you be willing to cash in some favors, Ralph?"

"If it means stopping Al Gore from becoming president? Fuck, yeah."

"Awesome. Joseph Lieberman, why don't you just return to Gore campaign headquarters and lay low for a while. You can still campaign and all, but maybe just try to take it a little easy. I hear you have some new screws, and I wouldn't want to see Gore pick up the sympathy vote if his V.P. loses his head on election day." To his collar, Dick whispered "Liebermanbot, execute one-ninety-four-dash-Y."

"Good luck, everyone. I am not a Republican." Joseph Lieberman grabbed his briefcase and walked out.

"Hey—you sure you can handle Plan B, Ralph? I mean, if my Plan A doesn't work out. Can get the Supreme Court on our side?"

"Oh, yeah. In the issue of Bush v. Gore, Scalia and Rehnquist are my little bitches. And heck—I'd say the same about Sandra Day. But she's a woman and I'm afraid someone would make a fucking gender issue out of it."

"Really?" asked Kimo. "Out of calling her your little bitch?"

"Listen. This is the 21st century we're dealing with here. Plus, I'm a lawyer. I know what I'm talking about."

"Even so, that's so weird that you'd catch flak about calling O'Connor your little bitch before calling Rehnquist that. I mean, he is the Chief Justice."

"I know, Kimo. But that's how it goes in the world today."

"Aren't we going to need more than just those three?"

"Yes, Dick. We'll need five. Now, we could luck out and have two naturally believe the case before them. But that's a touch risky."

"Hey, I could call Thomas and Souter. George the Elder picked those guys, so they owe him one."

"Alright, you call Thomas and Souter. I'll handle Scalia, Rehnquist, and O'Connor. That should do it."

"Hopefully, it won't come to that. If Plan A works."

"Alright, I better get going."

"Thank you, Ralph. I owe you one."

"That's how it works, Dick. And don't think I won't cash it in sometime."

Dick smiled. "I know you will, Ralph. I know you will."

. . .

Stop and ask for directions, honey.

I don't get it. It should be right here. The inauguration.

Just stop and ask someone.

I don't understand—I set it for 2000 Gore inauguration, but I don't see a Democrat anywhere.

Admit it, we're lost. You're afraid to admit we're lost.

We're not lost!

I bet we'd be lost no matter where we went.

Will you stop—we're not lost.

Fine—how about if I say it's all my fault. You're not to blame at all. And so I better be the one to fix it.

Thank you.

So, stop the car. I'm going to ask this gentleman here for directions. Hey—stop the car.

Okay, fine. Look I'm stopping.

Excuse me, kind sir. Can you help us? We're looking for January 22, 2000—Al Gore's inauguration.

January 22 is right here—well, actually it's tomorrow. So you've found that. But tomorrow is George Bush's inauguration.

But—but that's impossible.

No, mam.

Oh, this is bad, honey. Let me think.

What?

No Gore presidency. No Dash-Chose scandal. No under-assistant deputy position for you. I hope you're not too upset.

Nah, I never really cared for politics, anyway. Although…wait a second…Huh. You know, now that I stop to think about it, I think I might have been President not too long ago.

Really? You're serious?

Yeah, I think it goes back to the Bush presidency. His VP is Dick Cheney, who helps select Donald Rumsfeld as secretary of defense and when Rumsfeld resigns midway through Bush's second term—he's replaced by this Gates fella, and then oh! Let me just jump ahead: I become president in 2496!

Oh, honey! I'm so happy for you! I guess sometimes things just work out better than expected. Yes—now that I stop to think, I seem to recall hosting quite a lovely event for that Olympic curling team. It was so nice!

Yes, one of your better parties.

Hey! Look behind us. The Secret Service.

I was wondering about them back there.

You mean you saw them following us? Why didn't you say anything?

I didn't want to scare you—I mean, you have to admit that's a pretty mysterious looking car. We can't even see through the glass.

Well, anyway. Wow—I'm so excited, honey! I'm the former first lady! I think the media still has to call me the first lady, though. Ah, those were such good times. I'm sorry it all ended in you being just the third president to resign, after the whole arms-for-arms scandal.

Hey—bygones. It's water under the kryiqaduk as far as I'm concerned. But I'll say again what I said to that commission. It was absolutely the right thing to do at the time, trading our useless munitions and warheads for prosthetic arms to give to poor paraplegic inner city kids. I would do it again.

Let's go home, honey.

Great idea, dear.

.　　.　　.

From the Journal of Dick Cheney

November 7, 2000

8pm. They've called Florida for Gore. Not good. My plan is totally based on winning Florida, even if by one vote. Here I worked it all out and realized that if we take the most electoral votes, then we'd win. Yes, the plan is to take more electoral votes than Gore. Winning the popular vote may be how you win elections in those backward third-world countries—hell, it may even be how it happens in every other country on earth for all I know. But this is the U.S. of A. And here, we have something called the Electoral College. I'm not exactly sure how it works. Hillyer explained it once in history class, but I do know more electoral votes equals victory.

10:20pm. Okay, they've uncalled Florida for Gore. Maybe things aren't as bad as I thought. You'll be alright, Dick. Just don't worry too much—your heart might not be able to take it. What to do, what to do? I got it. I'll call Tony over at Fox and ask him to call it for George. Because if one network calls it, the others follow suit, not wanting to appear that they missed something. Yes, I'll make the call. Nah, better have George or Jeb call—after all, he's their cousin.

Shit, I thought this was foolproof. But now I may be the fool. Yeah, I had the plan, but I should have spent more time figuring out the execution? I probably couldn't beat Al Gore in a presidential election if my life depended on it. Shit.

2am. Yes. Victory! George's cousin at Fox calls it. All the other networks did just as I suspected. Thanks, Tony. I owe you one. Or rather, George owes you one.

3:30am. Well, maybe not. Al Gore unconcedes. What kind of asshole unconcedes? God, I bet that's not even a word. This is all messed up. I'm going to bed.

November 17, 2000

Sorry I haven't written more, dear diary. But there hasn't really been much to report. Election night came and went. They said Gore took more votes. But of course it was never my plan to get more votes. There is still hope. Florida is still up in the air and if we win Florida, we can call it a day. Then no more lectures from dad.

I'm not sure what I'll do if we lose. Sure, I could go back to 2791, but I've developed a life here. Lynne, the kids. I mean, I guess I'll be around in the future anyway—I'll be born there, after all. So even if I die having never gone back, at least I'll still see Natrona again.

December 10, 2000

Tomorrow's the big court case, Bush v. Gore, to settle the score. And, it sure was a good thing George's dad had the opportunity to fill two slots for that Supreme Court. So this is what it comes down to and you never know when you're going to need to call in a favor. Now, to make the calls...

Dammit! My phone died! I totally forgot to charge it. Shit, shit, shit. I've got to find a landline. Not good, not good. And why am I still writing???

December 12, 2000

That was too close. I actually never got through to either Souter or Thomas. I did leave a message with Judy at the Supreme Court switchboard to let her know Dick Cheney was calling and to please ask Justices Souter and Thomas to vote for Bush, if they got the message before the big case. But she said they had already gone in. Though she did say if they stepped out for a break before the decision, she'd try to get them the message. But there was no break. I was freaking out, and with good reason. Thomas voted for George, but Souter totally voted against him! Nader did got through to Rehnquist, O'Connor, and Scalia, and fortunately, Kennedy came out of nowhere and voted for George. Not sure who he owed, but no matter. Victory is ours.

The Court said something funny about how the decision pretty much applies only to this case and can't be taken as a general rule of law. What did they say? Here it is: "Our consideration is limited to the present circumstances." Can they do that? I mean, aren't they saying that a rule is a rule, except in this very particular case? That's messed up. Sure I wanted them to vote for us, but I'd think such smart people could come up with better arguments. Maybe something more complicated so it isn't so easy to take apart. But I can't look a gift horse in the mouth. This means the statewide recount stops. And if they don't examine the votes to certify whether we *really* won, well, that means we really won.

I'd love to call Gore now and just keep saying "We win! You lose! We win! You lose!" George says we should be gracious in victory, but I don't think he fully appreciates the situation. I mean, the guy caused all the pain and suffering in the world. Unless Hillyer is right and he actually spared the world much of its pain and suffering. Regardless, the guy was a thorn in my side from the time I learned to talk. Or rather, learned to listen. Funny. I can no longer remember the rants about Gore—did they actually happen? Well, wherever you are, Dad, this one's for you.

December 14, 2000

I confirmed that George the Elder called Thomas. George did set the guy up with a cushy lifetime gig—a pretty nice pay package, a goodly amount of prestige, and a snazzy robe, to boot. So what else is he gonna do when he has to decide whether George's son should be President? But I still come back to the question of Kennedy: Why? Unless he owed someone else a favor, of course. But who?

I'm going to cherish this for a while, but I also know I better start figuring out the rest of my life, or else I'm going to be coasting on the one accomplishment I've worked most of my adult life for.

I did talk with Rummy about the whole replicate-the-Stanford-prison-experiment-but-with-an-entire-country thing. He has some great ideas about how we can throw out the rule of law and really have fun with it. So there's that.

. . .

On a Wednesday night in December 2000, then-U.S. Vice President Al Gore stood with his wife Tipper, his fellow candidate Liebermanbot, and other friends and family. And he conceded.

Tonight, said Gore, for the sake of our unity of the people and the strength of our democracy, I offer my concession.

I promised him, said Gore, that I wouldn't call him back this time. I offered to meet with him as soon as possible so that we can start to heal the divisions of the campaign and the contest through which we just passed.

He said: Neither he nor I anticipated this long and difficult road, certainly neither of us wanted it to happen. Yet it came, and now it has ended. Resolved, as it must be resolved, through the honored institutions of our democracy.

He said: Let there be no doubt, while I strongly disagree with the court's decision, I accept it. I accept the finality of this outcome which will be ratified next Monday in the Electoral College.

He said: Almost a century and a half ago, Senator Stephen Douglas told Abraham Lincoln, who had just defeated him for the presidency: 'Partisan feeling must yield to patriotism.' Well, in that same spirit, I say to President-elect Bush, that what remains of partisan rancor must now be put aside.

And he said: May God bless his stewardship of this country.

. . .

On a Saturday night in January 2001, George Bush stood with his wife Laura, his fellow candidate Dick Cheney, and other friends and family. And he gave his inaugural address.

The peaceful transfer of authority is rare in history, said Bush, yet common in our country. With a simple oath, we affirm old traditions and make new beginnings.

As I begin, said Bush, I thank President Clinton for his service to our nation; and I thank Vice President Gore for a contest conducted with spirit and ended with grace.

We have a place, he said, all of us, in a long story. A story we continue, but whose end we will not see. A story of flawed and fallible people, united across the generations by grand and enduring ideals.

He said: Sometimes in life we are called to do great things.

He said: I will live and lead by these principles, "to advance my convictions with civility, to pursue the public interest with courage, to speak for greater justice and compassion, to call for responsibility and try to live it as well." In all of these ways, I will bring the values of our history to the care of our times.

He said: We are not this story's author, who fills time and eternity with His purpose. Yet His purpose is achieved in our duty, and our duty is fulfilled in service to one another. Never tiring, never yielding, never finishing, we renew that purpose today; to make our country more just and generous; to affirm the dignity of our lives and every life.

And he said: God bless you all, and God bless America.

Nearby, Dick Cheney smiled. And thought to himself, Damn, this was a long time coming. But well worth the effort.

He thought: I can't wait until my future childhood when I won't have to sit through so much as one lecture on the terrible no-good very bad Gore presidency. No more of Dad's rants.

And he thought: Man, will he be proud of me.

Epilogue

A man sits in a chair, a half-empty beer to his side. Nearby stands a younger man—no, he is a boy. Obviously a teenager though he appears more confident. Perhaps a football player or a wrestler, he carries himself like a man. The boy looks at his ball but is clearly listening as the man rages at his newspaper.

"I tell you, son. This all started well before your time. Centuries ago, with that god-damn-forsaken, no-good, good-for-nothin' George Bush. That's when the party went to shit. I'm almost ashamed to call myself a lifelong Republican. 'Party of Liebermanbot,' my ass."

The man drains the bottle before tossing it at the wall a few feet from the boy's head. The boy is not startled by the pop against the wall or the falling rain of glass. He turns away, but the man stops him. "Promise me, son. If you ever get the chance to save the world from that Bush presidency, that you'll do it."

The boy is unsure if the lecture is over.

"Promise me!"

The boy pauses. "I promise." The last words we hear from him, they somehow defy his stature. A body that exudes strength, confidence; a voice of reserve. Withholding something?

"What's that? Speak up, goddammit."

"I promise!" Almost shouting, before teeth clench tight.

The man laughs. "You're a good kid, Dickie. Yeah. You're a good kid alright."

.　.　.

Sir, the latest vote is in, said Lackey #4.

Hell, I thought we just had an election. Has it been six years already?

No, sir. You're just visiting us five years in the future. You were out of Post-It notes; you stopped in for office supplies.

Yes—well which is it? The Western Schism of 3119? Or maybe the potato famine has finally taken it. Ha! I jest.

No, sir. It's the 2004 election of John Kerry over George Bush. It was running neck and neck with the concept of Democracy, but once the votes from North Korea, Burma, and Canada came in, the election won handily.

God, I hate this job, he said. Another bloody election? Well, get me Agent Diebold this time. He'll be able to fix this.

Yes, sir.

And while you're at it, call Agent Blackwell. Send him to Ohio, just to be sure. I don't want to see this messed up.

No Apple pie this time, sir?

Hmmm…get her on the line. But this time, Lackey #4?

Yes, sir.

Call her personal line.

.　.　.

For those of you who purchased this book expecting much more Paris Hilton—that is her there in the title, after all —I must apologize. You see, this was never really about her. But I have good news for you. Because Ms. Hilton was not vaporized during any Gore administration, she continues to live on in the present. You can find her on television programs like *The World According to Paris*, and (I'm guessing here) probably everywhere else if you bother to look. But if you still need just a *wee* bit more, I leave you with this:

Eight years to the day after Paris *would* have been vaporized—had Dick Cheney not succeeded in subverting Al Gore's attempt to become president—I received a plain brown package in the mail. There was no return address, but the contents made the sender clear enough. The package contained one bottle of Heir cologne for men and one 8x10 photograph, autographed.

These were my rewards from the Paris Hilton Creative Best Friend Forever Contest. I had entered a photograph of me at the Del Norte County Fair, in which I had removed an image of my son and added one of Paris (sorry, Ro). I can't say it was my best design work, but it was apparently enough to earn an Honorable Mention.

For saving Paris, allowing her to live another day and host this contest, I would like to dedicate my bottle of Heir cologne for men to Dick Cheney, time traveling super hero. And here I definitely mean the character in this book—not former Vice President Cheney.

Thank you, Dick.

. . .

Dick Cheney, time traveling super hero

Mr. Richard Bruce "Dick" Cheney, passed away Saturday the 3rd after suffering his 13th heart attack. He was 123, having lived during the years 2754-2791, 1969-2011, and 2789-3033. He is survived by wife Lynne, daughters Elizabeth Perry and Mary Cheney, father Richard Herbert, five grandchildren, seventeen great grandchildren, fourteen great-great grandchildren, seven great-great-great grandchildren, twelve great-great-great-great grandparents, and one half-ninth cousin twice removed.

Most notable was when he saved the entire world from fairly certain destruction. While vacationing in the 20th century, Cheney visited 2000 and single-handedly reversed the outcome of the presidential election, bringing victory to George Bush over Al Gore. Historians, economists, scientists, activists, religious people, and business interests remembered the Gore presidency fondly, but it was later determined by the research subsidiary of Fox-RCAOLGE/Microsoftiburton that the root of all pain and suffering in the world was late in Gore's first term when celebrity socialite and hotel heiress Paris Hilton was accidentally vaporized during her attempt to visit a young Nicole Ritchie circa 1993.

Later in life, his memoir, *Captain Dick Saves the World: The Journal of Dick Cheney*, became a best-selling self-help book, with its strong message of placing higher education before partying, at least chronologically. A revised 544-page version was accidentally transported to August 2011, where it was released under the title *In My Time: A Personal and Political Memoir*.

Those wishing to pay respects can visit Thornton Funeral Home in Natrona Monday through Wednesday, 6-9pm. A private burial will be Thursday morning. In lieu of flowers, the family requests donations be made to Cheney's half-ninth cousin twice removed, the noted author Ryan Forsythe.

.　　.　　.

The End

In the future, everyone will vote to eradicate everything that has happened in the past, present, and future.

It has been hypothesized that one million or so monkeys stuck in a room with one million typewriters forever will eventually produce a complete play of William Shakespeare. The point is not that the monkeys will become bored of screeching or perhaps typing nonsense and eventually get down to the hard work of writing something good. The idea is that the random pressing of buttons for infinity will eventually result in any and all series of button presses, including *Hamlet* or that Scottish play. But if one million monkeys can produce a work of Shakespeare, perhaps this demonstrates that random is maybe not so random after all.

By the same token, given enough time—say, the rest of time—eventually personkind will get around to voting to do away with everything that has ever happened.

They will vote to do away with assassination, pogroms, manslaughter, suicide, and genocide. They will stamp out racism, sexism, chauvinism, agism, plagiarism, fascism, and capitalism. And then they will vote to exterminate dirt, disease, virus, bacteria, and mercury in children's vaccinations.

They will vote to get rid of bigotry, hatred, and fear, as well as hippies, yippies, preppies, yuppies, buppies, and scuppies. Many of them will never have heard of scuppies, but that won't stop them from voting.

Gone will be insurance premiums and seasonal-affective disorder. Limburger cheese, liverwurst, and Live-AID. Cover bands, genetically modified corn, and doing things for a Klondike bar.

They will eject fast food, Woodstock anniversary concerts, self-publishing, and democracy.

It's a slow process, with one event disappearing every six years. But after a few thousand years, they will become rather efficient in this voting thing. In 7823, the vote will be to do away with the decade from 3872 to 3881. Yes, the vote was six years in the making, but ten years will be gone in a snap. It won't be until the 10660's that they start doing away with entire centuries.

Eventually everyone will have the same abilities, skills, opportunities, choices. They will have the same language, logic, judgment, beliefs, and knowledge. And they will have the same mind-numbing boredom.

They will then vote to eliminate this boredom. But it won't work. For unlike seasonal-affective disorder, boredom is not something that can just be voted away with a one-time ballot of all the people of the earth.

The people will never vote to eliminate determination, fortitude, purpose, and hope. But these will be gone anyway.

And so they will vote to no longer vote. But in the final vote, this idea—to eradicate the vote on what to eradicate from the past—will take second place.

Instead, the winning vote in 14920 will be to do away with time itself, the universe, everything.

.   .   .

After the final vote but well before its implementation, one brave soul will venture back to the year 2011, in order to warn humankind of the impending danger. This traveler will fear institutionalization or worse if he is too forward with his bizarre but very true tale. Naturally he will hide the information in a book, knowing intelligent readers will get the message and take action. This book, *Dick Cheney Saves Paris*, is now available from Love Earth Publications. If you are able to read this, there is still hope.

Still *time.*[*]

---

[*] Cue closing theme, "Right Now" by Kevin Conaway, from the Love Earth Music soundtrack *music from and inspired by the novel Dick Cheney Saves Paris*.

No. I cannot expect you to believe it. Take it as a lie — or a prophecy. Say I dreamed it in the workshop. Consider I have been speculating upon the destinies of our race until I have hatched this fiction. Treat my assertion of its truth as a mere stroke of art to enhance its interest. And taking it as a story, what do you think of it?

— THE TIME TRAVELLER
from *The Time Machine*
by H.G. Wells

DICK CHENEY SAVES PARIS
BONUS MATERIALS

Deleted Epilogue

*Original Chapter One with Commentary
by Ryan Forsythe, Dick Cheney, and Skip Peterson*

About Dick Cheney

About Ryan Forsythe

*Genealogical Link Between
Dick Cheney & Ryan Forsythe*

Reading Group Guide

Coming Attractions

Deleted Epilogue

Like most deleted scenes from movies or books, the work below simultaneously gives deeper insight into the ideas of the creator while showcasing some of the work that, frankly, was not quite so good as to make the final cut. We make no claim to the quality of the work presented, but provide it so that you may gain a deeper appreciation for the craft and artistry of the author. Actually, let's go ahead and make a claim: this stuff is definitely not as good as the rest, so maybe don't read it. Why not do yourself a favor and skip ahead to the other bonus features.

By now you're noticing that the book is winding down and here I've barely covered any part of the Cheney (Vice) Presidency. And you're thinking, What gives?

As noted earlier, timeliness matters. This time, I'm placing a greater emphasis on getting it out the same day as Cheney's memoir, than on getting it right.

Can you blame me? I mean, do you think there's any chance that if I put a few hundred more hours into this book, that it would be any kind of bestseller? That thousands more people would rush to read it? If so, you have much to learn about the publishing world. So do I, of course.

If you want to know more about the Bush-Cheney administration, read a book. I've got things to do, songs to record, album ads to design. Have you heard? We're putting a soundtrack together.

music from and inspired by the novel
Dick Cheney Saves Paris

If you don't have your copy yet, let me take a second to leap forward to when it's all done and say, damn, look at this collection. Great artwork, a killer collection of tracks. And it's available now from Love Earth Music. I'm guessing there's an advertisement at the end of the book.

Speaking of the soundtrack, for those of you fortunate to already have a copy, you may have noticed that not all the tracks have been referenced as of yet. And if not all are mentioned, can we call the soundtrack songs *from and inspired by* the book? Of course, we can. I bet I can even remedy this in one paragraph. The key is that *as of yet*.

As I write, I am listening to (respectively) the theme song from the top of page 41 ("Sound of the Night" by Instagon),[*] the love theme from Feb 14, 1973 ("Passionfruit" by Jolthrower), the P-NAC Group theme song ("Searchers" by Cabron), Liebermanbot's theme ("Society" by the Incests), and the theme from sometime between the entries on page 203 ("Augusta '02" by Croatoan). Oh, and let's definitely not forget the interlude by Endometrium Cuntplow. That should cover it. Unless, of course, Steve at Love Earth adds a last-minute track to the album, in which case let's call it the theme

---

[*] Cue the song...oh, just go ahead and cue the whole damn soundtrack, *music from and inspired by the novel <u>Dick Cheney Saves Paris</u>*.

to Dick Cheney's kidney stone or something like that.

Anyway, this may be the last time I check in, so don't forget to check out that ad. Operators are standing by.

Gosh, I've grown so attached to you. Hopefully we can do this some other time, though next time can it be over your book?

Okay, I'll stop already. I'll let you finish up.

.   .   .

From the Journal of Dick Cheney

January 19, 2001

Today is the first day of the rest of the week. Sure, I got sworn in today as Veep. But I don't want to look at it like it's any more or less special than the other things I've been doing until now. Maybe it's that I don't have as much to live for, having accomplished what I'd been working toward for thirty odd years.

But Rummy and I have been making plans. And I think I have a new passion. We talked with George about Iran and Iraq and he couldn't tell them apart. He said we could play it safe and just say they all harbor terrorists—maybe throw in some other countries too, in case we later want to expand our little experiment. "How about that South Korea?" he asked. "They're pretty bad dudes, huh?"

Rummy was pretty sure that North Korea was the bad one, so he's going to Google it and get back to us. If so, we've got a plan to mention it in a speech somewhere down the road that all these countries are harboring evil people and they must be stopped. That should allow us to invade a few.

Rummy says the thing we have to watch out for is that people might think we're going there because they have a lot of oil and people might think we want to take it for ourselves. I think he's wrong—who could possibly think that? But just to be on the safe side, we'll be sure to mention in our speeches some other reason—like maybe that we need to bring democracy to the people.

September 11, 2001

Damn. I don't even know how to write about this, where to begin. Today was a terrible day for our nation, maybe even for all nations. Terrorists hijacked several planes and flew them into the two towers of the World Trade Center and the Pentagon. They even hijacked another with plans perhaps for the White House, but some brave people aboard fought their way into the cabin to wrestle control of the plane. They knew they were goners, but that didn't stop them from selflessly stopping the terrorists from taking out other targets, other people. But the towers collapsed killing thousands of people. It was eerie—they just fell straight down, collapsed in on themselves.

I don't really want to think about it at this time, but I do believe this will push back the little plans Rummy and I have for invading Iran or Iraq. Most of the terrorists were from Saudi Arabia. And on behalf of those who died, we may have to go there and tear the place up. But that's fine. Our little experiment can wait forever if need be. More important is to find those responsible and let the country begin the long slow process of recovery and healing.

My heart is filled with grief. It is a sad sad day.

September 13, 2001

So scrap what I said the other day. At least the part about Saudi Arabia. George says no can do. We can't go into Saudi Arabia because they're good friends with his dad. Something about lots of money and favors and oil and such. So we talked about it—George, Rummy, and I—and decided Afghanistan was our best bet. Word on the street is the hijackers were working for Al Qaeda or the Taliban or something, and I guess they have a big presence in Afghanistan. More important is the fact that their military has pretty much no real firepower. So we can go in and rip the place apart, which will show the world that we mean business. Don't mess with the U.S.

Colin kept wanting to know what we were talking about. "Come on, guys—you never tell me anything!" Reminded me of my days with Nixon, actually. Ah, memories. But he needs to understand that he's the Secretary of State, so it's not like any of this concerns him.

February 11, 2006

So I shot my hunting partner today Out shooting quail over in Kennedy County, I turn to fire, and there he is. I know, I know. So not cool. An honest accident.

Damn, this sucks. The guy suffered a minor heart attack. But hey—it's not like I haven't had my own share of heart attacks. I might be having one right now. In fact, if this guy knows what's good for him, he better apologize for the trauma he's caused *me*.

But hell, I'm the Vice President. I'll do what I want.

I haven't told George yet. But no worries.

February 13, 2006

Talked to George. He was a little perturbed. He was all like, "Don't take this the wrong way, but I'd kinda appreciate it if you could maybe let me know when these things happen, Dick—at least within the next few days, you know. I mean, if you want to, that is. Don't think I'm trying to tell you what to do or anything. I'm just saying I think it would be good if you include me in the loop. If you think that's appropriate, of course. But I understand if you think that might be a bad idea."

"George…" I said.

"Yes, okay. I'll shut up. Thank you, Dick."

November 5, 2006

I don't know how much longer I can do this. I'm really starting to miss my old life back in the 27th century. I think maybe it's that I've accomplished the big three in life: I defeated Gore, my little prison experiment with Rummy is pretty much over, and I've watched my kids grow up and develop their own lives. So I don't have much more to live for—at least not in this time period.

When Kimo and I were on our way to Nantes 1847, I totally thought I'd be gone a weekend. But here it's turned into almost forty years, mostly dedicated to making sure some guy didn't get elected president. And for what: So my dad wouldn't harangue me? I don't know if it was worth it, but I've done it. Hang the banner: Mission accomplished. But now what?

You know what, I quit. I'm telling George he can find someone else to finish out my term. I'm going home. I'm not sure how, but I've gotta get out of here.

November 7, 2006

There goes that idea. I finally convinced Lynne to go with me, and we took out a reverse mortgage in order to get a new Filby. I was showing it to Rummy, and he stepped in to check it out. I said, "whatever you do, don't press that button."

Well, he points at it and says, "This one?" But he wasn't wearing his glasses, so of course his finger hits it, the thing starts shaking and flies down the driveway. So he's on his way to 2782.

We'll have to make up something—we'll say he resigned or something. I'll have to find one of the ol' guys to bring in to finish out his term. Maybe I'll give Robert Gates a call.

It's probably for the best. I probably couldn't "resign" now anyway—would reflect poorly on my administration. So I'll wait it out—just a few more years until 2008 and then McCain will handily beat the Hillary/Obama ticket (if future history books are any indication) and then I can finally retire to the 27th century with Lynne.

.   .   .

In the past, literature popularized the concept of time travel.

Perhaps the most well known early novel to examine the idea of time travel was *The Time Machine* by H.G. Wells. With the publication of this book in 1895, time travel became something for young boys to fantasize about. Stepping into a machine and visiting a distant land was in the realm of possibility. But his was not the first tome to consider such an idea.

Prior to Wells, Charles Dickens had Ebenezer Scrooge

visit Christmas past, Christmas present, and Christmas yet to be. Though some argue they may have been simply dreams or visions and not actual time travel.

French geologist Pierre Boitard's *Paris before Men*, published in 1861, had its main character visit prehistoric times with the help of a magic demon. And no, the main character was not Paris Hilton.

Time travel also featured in Edward Page Mitchell's 1881 short "The Clock That Went Backward," though the first story to involve an actual time machine was probably "El Anacronpete" by Enrique Gaspar y Rimbau in 1887. *The Chronic Argonauts* by Wells appeared in 1888, the same year as Edward Bellamy's *Looking Backward*, in which the main character falls asleep and wakes up in the future.

Mark Twain's *A Connecticut Yankee in King Arthur's Court* appeared in 1889, followed two years later by *Tourmalin's Time Cheques* by Thomas Anstey Guthrie. And that doesn't even get us to 1900.

Over the last century, the time travel stories have come faster and faster. And it's not just fiction authors tackling the subject. Philosophers, scientists, travel writers, screenwriters, and many others have shared their ideas on time travel.

It appears that if it can be written about, it can be a method of traveling to the future or past: an affliction, falling asleep, hypnosis, the help of magic demons, large machines that people step into, even sitting on an airplane.

But in the annals of time travel literature, only one work demonstrates the ability of yogurt to power travel through time.

ORIGINAL CHAPTER ONE
WITH COMMENTARY

The book was initially broken into approximately 50 chapters, before being reorganized in later drafts. Below is the original draft of Chapter One, compete with the "lost" commentary, recently discovered in an attic in Peoria, Illinois, and dated to November 2006. At that time, author Ryan Forsythe apparently sat down with star Dick Cheney and editorial assistant Skip Peterson.

ONE

Buds

On a simmering afternoon in late August, 2791, Richard Bruce "Dick" Cheney was out playing bocce with his bestest buddy ever, Kimo.

RF: I guess we should begin by introducing ourselves. So hi, I'm Ryan Forsythe, author of this novel.

SP: Hi, I'm Skip Peterson. I did the copy-editing and the layout for this chapter.

DC: And this is Dick Cheney, Vice President of the United States.

RF: And you are now reading the commentary for chapter one. Okay, so here you see the big ONE.

DC: I'd just like to start, Ryan, by saying that I loved your chapter

"Man, these are good times. Pass me another, would ya?"

"You said it, Dick." Kimo clicked open the Beer-On-Demand 20,000 and set the dial to "Bud." The machine whirred into action. After 72.4 seconds, the bottle dropped into the Tolzi box and Kimo tossed it over.

Dick eyed the bottle. "I think your clock is busted, Kee. It says the born-on-minute is 16:35:17.1, but I bet it's not even 4 o'clock yet."

"Yeah, I've been meaning to get it looked at. But hell—if it's in the shop, then fuck—no beer!"

"I hear you, bro. No worries." Dick took a swig. "Say—you wanna head to Peachtree for the long weekend?" Clinton Day was Monday, honoring the nation's first female president, so everyone had the day off. Sure, there had been several female presidents in the 740+ years since 2048 when

subheading for this.

RF: Early on, I wasn't sure what I was going to go with on this chapter—I was thinking maybe something about friendship. But then it hit me. The double meaning of the friendship and the beer. It was a natural.

DC: It just works so well.

SP: Yeah, good choice.

DC: Can I ask you, Ryan, was it difficult coming up with the concept for the novel?

RF: Not really. I started with the idea of you, Dick, as a sort-of superhero from the future who comes back to change time. As I worked with it, I decided it worked on many more levels to have you as the accidental, maybe even reluctant, superhero—a partier who, while he ends up saving the world, does so for perhaps not the most noble of causes.

DC: I think this made it a more fun role to play, as well. I've played so many parts where it's all positive—the character doesn't have a weakness. But here you made the character so complex, so multi-dimensional.

RF: Well, it made it very easy for me to write knowing that you could handle it. We should tell

Chelsea became not only the first female president, but the first single, unmarried president. A movement for the bicentennial in 2248 made the date a permanent holiday.

"Oh, sorry. I forgot to ask you. My bro is out of town, so he said I could borrow his Filby. I was actually thinking of checking out Firenze 1481 or perhaps Nantes 1847. Wanna come with? We could always hit Peachtree next month."

Dick smiled. "Dude, you've been wanting to go to Nantes for years and years, but something always comes up. What makes you think you'll actually make it this time? Why don't we just hit Stebold 2772?"

"Nah, man. High school is a thing of the past. You need to move on."

"Well, Nantes 1847 is even more past."

"You're stupid."

"No, you're stupid."

people this is the first time we've worked together.

DC: First time.

RF: But having seen your work before, I knew you could handle the range.

SP: We're coming up on a point, Ryan, that I know was a little different in an earlier draft. You changed it from "Do you wanna come with me?" to "Wanna come with." Maybe you can talk about your choice of language and how you make decisions like this.

RF: Oh, sure—by the way, we just saw the first reference to Nantes 1847.

DC: Though not the last.

RF: Yes, we'll see that again. By the way, right there I thought your performance was quite understated, Dick. Just a simple smile. It conveyed so much.

DC: That's what a great writer can bring out of a character.

RF: But back to "Wanna come with?" it just sounded more true, you know? That's the important thing to me. As I recall, Skip, you wanted to change it to "Do you want to?" but I fought you on this one. Not that your approach would have been wrong. But this fits more with the vision I had for

"I'm not the 37-year-old with the hots for a 17-year-old."

"Hey—Katie Driscoll is not 17. She's the same age as us."

"True." Kimo sipped his Bud. "But you don't want to go to Stebold 2791."

Dick had been to 2772 a few weeks earlier, but wasn't sure he wanted Kimo to know yet. Even though Katie Driscoll totally hated his guts in high school, she was developing a crush on 2791 Dick. But that's not the type of thing Kimo could ever let him live it down. So he let it drop. "How about Chouli in 3416?"

"Dude, Chouli hasn't happened yet, so how the hell would we know if it was worth checking out? Besides, I heard there were some fine-ass bitches in Nantes 1847."

"Sure, Kimo. Count me in."

More than spending time with Kimo, Dick was the character.

DC: It also made it feel more natural interacting with the Kimo character.

SP: Did anyone notice how this chapter was set in Garamond 12pt?

RF: Um, yeah. Anyway.

DC: I know we don't see this in this chapter, but I thought it was quite interesting that you chose to have alternating chapters focus on different characters—different aspects of the story. It wasn't all told from Dick's perspective.

RF: Well, a writer needs to constantly challenge himself or herself. My previous novels were pretty much first-person accounts from the same person for the whole book. I really wanted to try something a little more challenging.

DC: Plus, every third chapter as a mini history lesson—those were some of my favorite parts.

RF: Hey—Chouli 3416! There it is.

DC: Do we ever learn what happens in Chouli 3416? I don't think we do.

RF: Sequel! I'm kidding. But seriously, I do think some things are better left to the imagination. I don't want to give too much to the looking forward to another weekend away from his old man and his eternal "If you ever get a chance to save the world..." lectures. God, they sucked total ass. If his dad had so much as one ounce of booze, he was off and running on his favorite topic.

They made plans to meet the next day at the D & P. Then they drank some more Bud.

reader.

DC: And here is the chapter's lone reference to Dick's father's lectures.

RF: Yeah, it was important that we set up early the reason for the whole novel—not why he goes back in time, but why Dick goes forward in time, what motivates him.

DC: But you don't reveal too much. We don't know here what the lectures were really about. Was that on purpose?

RF: Absolutely. It was definitely purposeful to not include too much. I wanted to draw the readers in, get them to keep turning the page.

SP: Looks like we're out of time, gentlemen. But hopefully people will keep turning the page.

RF: But this is at the end of the book, so probably not (*DC & RF laugh*). Anyway, thanks for reading, everyone. Any final thoughts, Dick?

DC: Just to say the war on terrorism must continue. That's all.

SP: Bye.

ABOUT DICK CHENEY

Dick Cheney was born January 30, 1941 in Lincoln, Nebraska. He grew up in Casper, Wyoming, and earned his bachelor's and master of arts degrees from the University of Wyoming. In 1964, he married Lynne Vincent. They have two daughters. His political career began in 1969 when he joined the Nixon administration. He has served under four presidents, including as Chief of Staff to President Gerald Ford. Additionally, he served as the lone congressman from Wyoming, having been elected six times. In the House, he served as Chairman of the Republican Policy Committee, Chairman of the House Republican Conference, and House Minority Whip. In 1989, President George H.W. Bush selected him as Secretary of Defense. In this position, he directed Operation Desert Storm, for which he was awarded the Presidential Medal of Freedom. In 1995, he became Chairman and CEO of Halliburton Corp., a position he quit in order to run for Vice President of the United States.

ABOUT RYAN FORSYTHE

Ryan Forsythe was born January 25, 1973 in Cleveland, Ohio. He grew up in Cleveland, Ohio and earned his bachelors degrees from the Ohio State University and his masters degrees from Indiana University and Humboldt State University. In 2000, he married Kaci Elder. They have two sons. Like Dick Cheney, he never served in the military, but he believes he is the only person in the world present at both AWP in Denver when Lidia Yuknavitch stuffed a page of a Gideon's bible in her mouth and shot it in the general direction of Davis Schneiderman, and at The Shot, when, during the fifth and final game of the first round of the 1989 NBA playoffs, Michael Jordan launched the ball over Craig Ehlo at the buzzer to win the game and the series. In 2011, he entered the Paris Hilton Creative BFF Contest, for which he was awarded Honorable Mention. In 2004, he became Production Line Manager for CustomFlix, an Amazon company, a position he quit in order to help run Redwood Hostel.

Genealogical Link Between Dick Cheney & Ryan Forsythe

Joanna Lowell – Dick Cheney

Percival Lowell married Rebecca Lowell,

their daughter Joanna Lowell married (2nd) Capt. William Gerrish,

their son Moses Gerrish married Jane Sewell,

their daughter Jane Gerrish married Samuel Swett,

their son Samuel Swett married Elizabeth Adams,

their daughter Elizabeth Swett married William Cheney,

their son Ebenezer Cheney married Hannah Eaton,

their son Elias Eaton Cheney married Lucy Fletcher,

their son Samuel Fletcher Cheney married Ella Phillips,

their son Thomas Herbert Cheney married Margaret Ellen Tyler,

their son Richard Herbert Cheney married Marjorie Dickey,

and their son is Richard Bruce "Dick" Cheney.

Joanna Lowell – Ryan Forsythe

Percival Lowell married Rebecca Lowell,

their daughter Joanna Lowell married (1st) John Oliver,

their daughter Mary Oliver married Samuel Appleton,

their son Oliver Appleton married Sarah Perkins,

their daughter Hannah Appleton married Dr. Thomas Swaine,

their daughter Margaret Swaine married Major John Bacheller,

their son Thomas Bacheller married Lucy Bartlett,

their son George Bacheller married Nancy Pond,

their son Ira Bartlett Bacheller married Mary Martin,

their son Clarence Bacheller married Elizabeth Belle Hanchett,

their son Gail Bacheller married Selma Anderson,

their daughter Thelma married William E. Forsythe,

their son Bob married Peggy Ryan,

and their son is Ryan Forsythe.

A
LOVE EARTH PUBLICATIONS
READING GROUP GUIDE

Dick Cheney
Saves Paris

Ryan Forsythe

A Conversation With The Author Of
Dick Cheney Saves Paris

Love Earth Publications sat down for an exclusive interview with *Dick Cheney Saves Paris* author Ryan Forsythe. If you have further questions not covered below, you can join the conversation at www.facebook.com/DickCheneySavesParis.

Love Earth Publications: Why did you decide to write a novel based around Dick Cheney?

Ryan Forsythe: It started with me wondering why on earth he did some of the things he did. For some reason, I imagined him as a sort-of anti-hero from the future trying to get home and doing whatever he could to get more yogurt for his time machine, even willing to vote against releasing Nelson Mandela from prison, though perhaps unaware of the ramifications of his actions. I wrote it in 2006, but then I shelved it and moved on to other things.

LEP: What caused you to revisit the book? Why now?

RF: It's all in the book. Haven't you read it? (*laughs*) In January 2011, I learned Cheney's memoir would be out come August. I began to think this might be my one chance to do something with the book. The one time it could be "timely"—otherwise it would remain hidden away in the recesses of my computer. Later that week, I learned Stephen Elliott and Eric Martin would be releasing *Donald*, their fictional account of Donald Rumsfeld undergoing torture in his own prison system. Seeing that someone else had a somewhat similar project, in the very moment I was reflecting on it, confirmed my plan. Especially as it was an author I respect. Prior to *Donald*, Elliott had released some fine political writing, as well as his innovative *Adderall Diaries*.

LEP: Your novel employs a variety of techniques, styles, and genres. There's genealogy, congressional hearings, newspaper articles, the past/present/future "history" lessons. You've got slapstick and sci-fi and political satire. Plus, the whole meta-fictional component. So, question: Where would I find this at a bookstore?

RF: Well, you probably wouldn't find it at all. (*both laugh*) Maybe some cool indy bookstore somewhere. Or perhaps a used bookstore, if readers are trying to get rid of it. But of course the best place to find it is the Love Earth website.

LEP: Ah, Thanks for the plug! How do you think writing a fictional memoir compares to writing straight biography?

RF: It's easier. I don't have to be as accurate with my facts. Which might be ironic, considering how I take politicians somewhat to task in the book for being a bit free with facts. But I'm not calling this nonfiction, so of course I think I have more leeway. Perhaps all nonfiction authors should call their works fiction. Clearly more fiction authors need to stop calling their works nonfiction.

LEP: What do you hope readers will come away with after reading *Dick Cheney Saves Paris*?

RF: My hope is that they won't think this is just a simple joke. Yes, I am liberal with the jokes and I do hope it is entertaining. But at the end of the day, I want them to think about political memoirs, like Cheney's *In My Time*, and I want them to question the stories we all hear. At the end of the day, Cheney's memoir is perhaps just as fictional as my version.

LEP: What do you say to people who think overt political writing doesn't have a place in so-called "literary fiction"?

RF: People who say such things will name Shakespeare or Charles Dickens and say they wouldn't have lasted if they were overtly political, but surely that ignores what they were doing at the time they were writing. My guess is the people who say such things don't read very much. At San Diego State, I've been working with Professor Hal Jaffe. He discusses socially conscious literature in his book *Beyond the Techno-Cave: A Guerrilla Writer's Guide to Post-Millenial Culture*. Another writer I've been fortunate to work with is Corey Lewis at Humboldt State. He has an essay called "The Pen & The Sword," in which he examines the long history of using literature to effect a change in society. I believe it is absolutely necessary for artists to use their voices to challenge the power establishment.

LEP: Are there other writers who influence you politically? Or who you can recommend for those of us wanting to read more socially conscious literature?

RF: Derrick Jensen would probably be pretty high up on my list. *A Language Older Than Words*, *Strangely Like War*, and *As the World Burns* are a few of his books well worth reading and re-reading. As a writing teacher, I've also combed his *Walking on Water* several times for ideas. As far as fiction goes, his book *Songs of the Dead* has probably had a direct influence on this project. Just about everything he writes is extremely powerful, with a clear concern for life.

LEP: At the book's start, you get a page or two in and then call for a "do-over." Can writers do that? (*both laugh*)

RF: I wanted to draw attention immediately to the fact that this is a book, precisely because most books don't seem to do that. That is, if we allow Dick Cheney to lull us into his story, we begin to believe in it. We are manipulated into believing that it is Truth with a big *T*, that his version is not merely *his* version, but *the* version of events. And so, with this particular novel, I feel I must make it clear that my version is but one version if only to condemn a reality that allows us to believe in political memoirs as reality. And here I use Dick Cheney as an obvious example, but this is not something specific to him or his memoir. There's a saying attributed to Churchill that "History is written by the victors." The takeaway is that the so-called facts of history should be questioned. Obviously the same should be said of memoirs written by those in power.

LEP: Switching gears, I must say, the concept of a novel soundtrack is fairly unique. How did that idea come about?

RF: It's not that uncommon these days for a novelist to put together a list of songs to play while reading the novel. You an find such playlists on youtube and other places. I'm also familiar with several writer-musicians who have written soundtracks for their own novels. But I'm not that talented. I will say that I think an album of original songs for a novel, written and performed by various artists is pretty unique.

LEP: What gave you the idea to have a soundtrack for this particular novel?

RF: As you know, Love Earth began life as a music label, with legendary noise bands like +DOG+ and Instagon. With a great music label, it just seemed right that music should play a part in this. So I pitched the idea to Steve *(Love Earth Music founder Steve Davis)* and he loved it. Things snowballed, with a great group of artists coming on board. Most are not well-known, but they're all extremely talented musicians and songwriters.

LEP: Yeah, it's a great line-up. I love the variety of styles— metal, rap, folk, punk, noise bands, instrumentals—even bagpipes and a singing robot. In a way, it mirrors the wide variety of techniques and styles in the novel itself.

RF: Speaking of the singing robot, one of the more fun parts of the soundtrack has been the collaboration with musicians on songs "inspired by" the book. For example, in the novel I mention a reality TV show hosted by Regis Philbin. I had emailed a draft to several of the musicians, to give a better idea of what the book was about. Well, Satanic Puppeteer Orchestra was inspired to write a theme song for the reality TV show! I was then able to re-write the scene in the book, so in the final version you see Agent Thornton taking a break to sing along as SPO perform the song live for Regis and Paris. Other musicians, like Alan Rose, Jeph Preece, and Softer Hobby, used the book to directly influence their contributions, making the soundtrack truly "music from and inspired by" the novel. At the same time, there are several tracks inspired not by the book at all, but by Dick Cheney and his colleagues. The contributions from Lex One, Kevin Conaway, and Cabron! were written during the Bush-Cheney years; we were fortunate to be able to include them.

LEP: It's also cool to have a Love Earth Music compilation connected to the very first Love Earth Publications release. I think we have time for one more question, or we'll need to add four pages to the book. (*both laugh*) Do you have a favorite Dick Cheney quote?

RF: If space is limited—with this book I should probably say "time." If *time* is limited, then I'll give a quick answer: No. Though perhaps I would say his comment to Senator Leahy is one of the most memorable.

LEP: That may have been too short! But thank you for your time and best of luck with the book.

RF: Thank you. It's been fun.

Questions & Topics For Discussion

The following questions are provided to both enhance individual reading and invite group discussion of the novel. We hope these questions generate a stimulating dialogue with others and provide additional topics for consideration.

1. Ryan Forsythe begins his novel with a quote from Charles Darwin: "Believing as I do that man in the distant future will be a far more perfect creature than he now is, it is an intolerable thought that he and all other sentient beings are doomed to complete annihilation after such long-continued slow progress." What do you think is meant by this quote and how does it prepare the reader for the following pages?

2. Forsythe takes us on a journey through time, space, and politics for both Dick Cheney and himself. How does the fact that this is a fictional work, yet based in part on the life of one real person while also inclusive of details for another real person, alter your reading of the book?

3. At one point, Forsythe refers to "Amazon.com's general je ne sais pas" (p. 122). Discuss what is meant by this.

4. At another point, Forsythe draws several parallels between himself and Dick Cheney. For example, both are Aquarians with brothers named Robert. Does this make Cheney more of a sympathetic character? Why or why not?

5. Throughout the novel, several philosophical questions are raised regarding time travel. For example, "Should there be a tax on time travel, and how would it be collected? How would it be enforced?" (p. 68) Discuss one of these questions, or choose another from the text.

6. Much of Cheney's voting record as a congressperson is attributed to wanting to borrow the time machine of alien pinochle player Donald Rumsfeld. Is this the most plausible explanation for Cheney's votes? Why or why not?

7. The novel occasionally references robots. For example, Joseph Lieberman is presented as a secretly Republican robot who only acts when Cheney whispers into his own collar. Discuss what robots might have to do with the political establishment.

8. Forsythe wrote this novel because he was disturbed by the actions of politicians like Dick Cheney and also by the general indifference of the media and much of society. Is there a historical or personal figure whose life and work disturbs you just as profoundly?

ACKNOWLEDGMENTS

My deepest thanks to Kaci and the boys for your love and support always. A special thank you to publisher Steve for taking this on as your first full-length book project at Love Earth.

Also, thanks to Hal Jaffe for help with this manuscript and my other work at SDSU, and to others who read an early version of the novel and offered suggestions (and/or just read it): Suzannah Lambert Bowser, Chris Hall, Bob Forsythe Jr., and Jennifer Schneider.

A huge shout out to all the musicians who shared their artistry on the novel soundtrack, "music from and inspired by the novel *Dick Cheney Saves Paris*": Cabron, Kevin Conaway, Croatoan, +DOG+, Endometrium Cuntplow, Generation Welfare, The Incests, Instagon, Jolthrower, Lex One, Liver Cancer, Jeph Preece, Alan Rose, Satanic Puppeteer Orchestra, Softer Hobby, The Tigers, and Versa.

Finally, thanks to all the people who supported the novel on Kickstarter.com, most notably Bob & Lari Forsythe, the biggest cheerleaders the project could have. As for the rest of you, you know who you are, and I thank you. But so, too, will others know of your generosity. For you are[*]:

---

[*] Note: Backers at the Presidential level are italicized

Pat Albrecht, Jason and Maria Andersen, Rachelle Bendixen, Stacie Canacci and Jeff Kalniz, Louie Centanni, Brian Chaffee, J. C. Cohen, Samuel Cole, Kevin Conaway, Amy Cornell, *Donald and Wendy Elder*, The Elders in Denver, Kaci Faylee, Kenneth Fenter, Phil Fenter, Adele M. Fini (SPB Class of '87), Amanda Fiore, Jennifer Forbes, *Bob and Peggy Forsythe*, Rob Funk, Dean George, Risa Goehrke, Eirik Gumeny, Chris and Rose Bazan, Kathy Harley, Sabinita Henrichsen-Schrembs, Michelle Herold, James C. Holder, Bella Holmes, Katherine Kleinhans, Mur Lafferty, Steve L'Heureux, Vanessa Hwang Lui, Michele Madden, Voni Maldonado, The McClures, Daniel McGauley and Family, Nanette Mickle, Mary Miller, Sara Morrison, Mike Mulen, Sarah Page and Mark O'Hare, Jeff Parry, Amanda Pecsenye, Terry Pettijohn, RoBert Rochelle, Shane Roeschlein, Alan Rose, Rachel Royer and Michelle Marx, Scott Scharmann, Brittney Schramm, David Stacey, Beverly Steichen, Alex Strang, Mariah Waldvogle, Barbara Wein and Michael Whitehurst, Captain Methane himself (Dorcey Wingo), and last but certainly not least, The Walkleys—Shannon, Jolyon, Alden, and Dylan.

Thanks, everybody. Bawk! Bawk!

coming attractions

FROM LOVE EARTH PUBLICATIONS

RAW ZED & THE CONDOR

(REVISED EDITION)

THE CLASSIC NOISE NOVEL BY

GX JUPITTER-LARSEN

PLUS NEW WORKS FROM

GITANE DEMONE
S. DAVIS
CHRISTIE SCOTT

for more info, visit
LoveEarthMusic.com

enhance your *Dick Cheney Saves Paris*
experience with the official soundtrack

music from and inspired by the novel

featuring

Cabron - Kevin Conaway - Croatoan - +DOG+
Endometrium Cuntplow - Generation Welfare - The Incests
Instagon - Jolthrower - Lex One - Liver Cancer
Alan Rose - Satanic Puppeteer Orchestra
Softer Hobby - The Tigers - Versa

CD available now from LoveEarthMusic.com

Digital download available from
DickCheneySavesParis.bandcamp.com

**digital version features an exclusive
bonus track from Jeph Preece**

www.ingramcontent.com/pod-product-compliance
Lightning Source LLC
Chambersburg PA
CBHW020104180626
46812CB00006B/2462